the Feisty One

the Feisty One

Cami Checketts

Birch River Publishing
Smithfield, Utah
Published in the United States of America
Cover design: Christina Dymock
Cover photo: Photo by Forewer
Interior design: Heather Justesen
Editing: Daniel Coleman

Dedication

To my sweetheart of a friend, Christina Dymock. Thank you for being such an amazing example to me and pushing me to be a better writer and a better person. I love your spunky, happy personality and am constantly inspired by your hard work and dreams.

Introduction by Lucy McConnell

I've heard it said that some people come into your life and quickly leave—others leave footprints on your heart. Jeanette and Cami are two wonderful authors and women who have left their mark on my heart. Their overwhelming support, knowledge, and general goodness have pushed me forward as a writer and nurtured me as a friend. That's why I'm pleased to introduce you to their new and innovative series: The Billionaire Bride Pact Romances.

In each story, you'll find romance and character growth. I almost wrote personal growth—forgetting these are works of fiction—because the books we read become a part of us, their words stamped into our souls. As with any good book, I disappeared into the pages for a while and was able to walk sandy beaches, visit a glass blowing shop, and spend time with a group of women who had made a pact—a pact that influenced their lives, their loves, and their dreams.

I encourage you to put your feet up, grab a cup of something wonderful, and fall in love with a billionaire today.

Wishing you all the best,
Lucy McConnell
Author of *The Professional Bride*

The Billionaire Bride Pact

I, Maryn Howe, do solemnly swear that I will marry a billionaire and live happily ever after. If I fail to meet my pledge, I will stand up at my wedding reception and sing the Camp Wallakee theme song.

Chapter One

Maryn Howe pulled up to a massive wrought-iron gate. The imposing twelve-foot tall fence surrounding the property was partially hidden behind hundreds of lodge pole pines. They looked almost as intimidating in their grand stature as the well-built guard marching up to her window. Pretending she hadn't seen the man yet, she quickly dialed her editor and close friend, James, one more time. "Are you absolutely sure about this?"

"You're going to be fine. He's only injured a couple reporters... That we know of." James laughed. He was teasing her as usual, but her nerves were too frazzled to respond. "He invited you, remember?"

"That's what you keep claiming. But James, I've researched the heck out of this dude and he is the ultimate reclusive Richie. He hates the media. Why would he want me to interview him?" She tried to keep the whine out of her voice, but it was proving impossible.

The guard tapped on her window. She held up a finger and flung a pleading smile his direction before staring at her steering wheel to avoid holding eye contact.

"Because you're beautiful, fun, and a fabulous writer," James said. "Why do you think I chase you so hard?"

Maryn appreciated the vote of confidence, but James pursued her nonstop so she couldn't take his word as an unbiased opinion.

She kept insisting she wasn't ready for anything beyond friendship, but he still teased her about marrying him all the time.

"I thought you chased me for my car." He hated her green Volkswagon bug.

"Ha!" He laughed. "That sense of humor is what I'm talking about. You've got this, no worries."

"Thanks, James. I just keep second guessing this trip."

"Tucker Shaffer has never allowed media into any of his homes," James said. "Do you know how many reporters would give up their iPhones to meet this guy, let alone be invited into his lair?"

The big bad wolf's lair. That's exactly what she felt like. A little lamb going to the slaughter. She squared her shoulders, prepared for the battle. Fighting for this story was more important than her insecurities. She was going to ferret out all of Tucker Shaffer's secrets where no one else had been given even a glimpse of the man. Yet, she couldn't help but admit to one of her closest friends, "I'm scared, James."

"Liar. My girl is too tough to be scared. You've never been scared of anything in your life."

James thought he knew her so well, but he had no clue how many times she'd been scared as a young child raised by a single mom who worked every part of her tail off to try to secure them some kind of life. She should've called her best friend, Alyssa, with her one phone call before she faced the mystery that was Tucker Shaffer. The man who became famous as the inventor of Friend Zone, the social media site that had risen above Facebook, Twitter, and Instagram in only a few short years. He supposedly hated reporters and didn't care that his PR ratings were in the toilet. He was a stinking billionaire, why should he care about PR?

"He'll love you," James reassured her. "You know I do."

Maryn wished she could ignore that, but appreciated that James was always there for her. "I know you do."

"Hey. Just because he's a billionaire, don't you dare think of falling for him. I know all about your little billionaire bride pact, but you're meant for me."

"Who needs a man, I've got a career," she teased. James had their future planned out, but she wasn't sure if she would ever be ready for that future. She *was* sure she'd never complete an agreement made at summer camp before she was even in the market for a training bra. All the girls in their cabin had sworn to marry a billionaire. It was something to joke about now. She'd forced herself to become comfortable around wealthy people as she spent most of her days interviewing and interacting with them. James teased her that she had a chip on her shoulder, but she'd never made much effort to chisel it off.

The guard tapped on her window again. He did not look happy.

"Gotta go. Guard dog is getting impatient."

"Guard what—"

Maryn hung up, turned her ringer off because she knew James would call back and she needed to focus right now, and pressed the window button. Brisk Idaho air rushed in. How could it be this cold in October? She wanted to go back to California. "Hi," she said too brightly. "I have an appointment with Mr. Shaffer, Maryn Howe. Word is he's excited to meet me." She gave him a huge grin and stuck her hand out the window to shake.

The guard looked at her fingers then back at her face. He didn't take his hand off his weapon. He was tall and lean with short brown hair and dimples that showed even though he wasn't smiling. It was hard to take someone with dimples seriously, but the weapon and stern look in his grayish-blue eyes helped. She got the impression this was not just a slacker guard who played Farmville in his guard shack all day.

"Can I please see some identification?" he barked at her.

"Wow." Maryn yanked open her purse and fished around for her wallet. She found her driver's license and held it up for inspection. "Talk about a stiff," she muttered.

The guard didn't react to her comment. He studied her driver's license for long enough that her fingers almost froze then nodded. "Mr. Shaffer is expecting you. Stay on the main road and it will lead you to the estate."

"Yay for the estate." She pumped a fist.

The guard arched an eyebrow and *almost* smiled. Almost might have been stretching it, but his grip on the rifle loosened a fraction. Why would he have a big old rifle instead of a pistol? He looked like he was ready to hunt for bear or something.

"Yay for the hot girl going to meet the big guy," he muttered.

"What did you just say..." Maryn shook her head, certain she'd heard him wrong.

He saluted her with his gun and a wink before turning back to the gate house.

"Whew. Crazy." Maryn rolled up her window, put her license away, and cranked the heat. The gate swung open. She proceeded slowly through and followed the winding road through more pine trees than she'd ever seen in her life. They were straight and tall, reminding her of a military unit. She snickered. The guard at the front gate had been a piece of work. Why had he called his boss the big guy? Well, Mr. Shaffer was a big guy from the photos she'd seen, but that guard was off. She wondered if the boss/employee relationship was much different here than what she'd encountered at other interviews.

The Feisty One

The long ribbon of asphalt and enormous property stretched around her, reminded her that this guy was the ultra in Richies. What was she doing pretending she could hang with somebody like this? Being raised around wealthy people as the live-in maid's daughter, she knew her place well. She'd risen to the top of her profession because of her good writing skills, her humor, and a refusal to quit. She regularly interviewed and rubbed cheeks with famous and wealthy people, but the only two of that species she was comfortable around were Alyssa and her new husband, Beckham. Those two didn't really qualify as wealthy snots as they spent their time and money helping underprivileged children the world over.

Why had she been so excited when James secured her this opportunity? The whole interview suddenly seemed dumb, presumptuous, and far too intimate—flying into Idaho Falls and then driving the rented Mazda hours into the backwoods of Island Park to go to this wealthy dude's house and what... drag all of his secrets out that he'd never revealed to anyone? Rolling her shoulders, she forced herself to keep driving. She'd worked too hard for too long to miss out an opportunity like this. Tucker Shaffer's story could propel her into semi-stardom and probably a huge bonus on top of that.

She understood quickly what the guard dog had meant by "main road" as paved paths led off through the trees at different intervals. The road seemed to go on forever. It had to be over a mile before the house came into view, but "house" didn't seem like the correct word. It was a massive log cabin. Absolutely gorgeous and sprawling. Maryn fell in love at first sight. It was large enough it should've been ostentatious, but it fit so well with the forest and river in the background that it was just an extensive of their natural beauty.

She relaxed for a minute, hoping Mr. Shaffer was like his house—big and too expensive, but still comfortable and welcoming. Somehow she was getting a thorough tour of this beaut. She didn't love rich people, but she did love impressive architecture and design. Crazy that this was only one of his homes. Her research had revealed pictures of beautiful estates in Potomac, Maryland; Laguna Beach, California; and Grand Cayman.

She stopped her rented Mazda in the circle drive and popped out of the door. The wind cut through her light jacket. She shivered and wrapped her arms around herself. It was barely October and she'd left seventy-five degrees when she flew out of L.A. and it had been a respectable fifty when she landed in Idaho Falls. This may be the most beautiful property she'd ever seen, but why endure the cold this time of year when he could be in California or Grand Cayman?

At least she looked good with gray, skinny jeans tucked into high-heeled red boots and a detailed Levi jacket over a blousy floral shirt. She flipped her blonde curls, knowing attractiveness was a bonus when interviewing grumpy men. She hated to use that card, but sometimes a girl had to utilize whatever tricks she could.

She bounced up the steps and pressed the button. A uniformed butler came to the door. He was perfect—tall, gray-haired, and so starched she wasn't sure how he moved.

Maryn grinned and stuck out her hand. "Hi, Maryn Howe. I have an intimate chat scheduled with the lucky Mr. Tucker Shaffer." She knew she shouldn't tease, but this guy had it coming.

The butler gingerly pressed her fingers, not so much as raising an eyebrow at her lingo. "Pleasure, Miss Howe. Please come in to the study."

Maryn gawked at the foyer with three stories up and one down of stairs, windows, and open space. The woodwork was unreal and when she craned her neck around the grand staircase she caught a glimpse of what must be the main living area. Ooh, she had to check out this house more. The only television shows she ever watched were on the Home and Garden Network featuring amazing homes.

The study was tasteful with windows showcasing the never-ending trees outside. The sun shone brightly today, but Maryn almost found herself wishing for a snowstorm. It would be amazing to see that forest become a winter wonderland—if she could stay inside with a warm cup of cocoa. She was getting more than a little ahead of herself. There were claims that Tucker Shaffer had thrown reporters off his property before. She'd better make a fabulous impression if she wanted to stay long enough for cocoa and a snowstorm. She smiled. She could only be herself, and if he didn't like that, she could do the flight of shame back to L.A. At least then her toes would be warm.

The butler gestured to a leather armchair. "Please, sit. Mr. Shaffer will be up shortly."

"I'm sorry. I didn't catch your name, my friend," Maryn said.

His eyebrows arched before his face returned to its former expressionless shape. "Mr. Braxton, at your service, ma'am."

"Well, it's very nice to meet you, Mr. Braxton." He was a funny old guy, so stiff and proper. Just another reason Maryn disliked wealth, it made the hired help into zombies. She should know, her mother had been the perfect, little maid doing everything the master of the house wanted, a sickening amount of everythings. Maryn vowed she'd never be a servant or a master and had carved a career out of sweat and starvation, only taking help from her best friend, Alyssa, and Alyssa's Granny Ellie, may that saintly woman rest in peace.

7

"You as well, ma'am. Pardon me." He swept from the room.

Maryn wasn't sure if she'd offended him or not. She shrugged and instead of sitting like he'd asked, perused the room, taking in the stately furnishings and lack of feminine fluff. The pictures she had of Mr. Shaffer showed a well-built, attractive, thirty-something business kind of guy. This house and the staff she'd met so far screamed uppity, but there was something about the massive desk covered in papers and the books lining the perpendicular wall. She stepped closer and was pleased to see Cussler, Clancy, and Baldacci mixed in with business and finance nonfiction books. Nice.

For just a second, she dreamed of cuddling up in one of the overstuffed leather chairs next to the fireplace and reading a book. She just needed some snow, a cup of cocoa, and an invite.

"The reporter is here?"

Braxton nodded quickly.

Tuck gestured to himself. "I'm a sweaty mess, Brax." He'd come back from a long run and immediately gone to his gym to box, losing track of time as he slugged it out with a punching bag.

He was drenched in sweat and if the pinched expression on Braxton's face was any indication, he smelled as bad as he feared. "You've got to stall her, let me shower quick."

"Um, well."

Tucker couldn't help but smile. He loved seeing Brax disconcerted.

"What do you suggest I do?"

"Give her a tour of the house. No, wait, I'm supposed to do that." He was racking his brain to remember all the stuff his PR people told him. Why couldn't he have invented something like Apple or be a real estate investor? Nobody seemed to care that Steve Jobs or Donald Trump were jerks, but supposedly Tuck needed a welcoming image because Friend Zone was a social site.

"See if she likes books. Let her read for a few minutes."

"Books?"

"I don't know. Offer her tea and crumpets or something. What do I pay you for Brax?"

Braxton cracked a half smile. "Not very much, *sir*."

"Exactly. One of the few times I have people over and you need to do your job." Tucker smiled. Braxton was an adopted grandfather, a former family practitioner, and worth almost as much as Tucker because of the companies Tucker had started in the old man's name. Braxton and Johnson thought it was funny to play butler and guard when they had an unsuspecting guest and bet on which one of them was more believable.

"I will try."

Braxton pivoted to leave.

"Wait, Brax. What's she like?"

Braxton tilted his head to the side. "Different than expected. Snarky, warm, and very, very beautiful."

He walked away and Tuck sat there for a few seconds wondering what she'd done to make Braxton describe her as snarky *and* warm. Johnson was supposed to greet her at the gate, he thought about calling to get his friend's impression, but he didn't have time.

No matter how his PR people begged, he liked the life of a recluse. Well, not really a recluse as he had his three best friends. He'd gone through his teenage years as a chubby foster child. None of his families seemed to dislike him, but no one but Braxton had ever cared much about him either. He despised people who thought he was someone to fuss about now that he'd grown a foot, shed the fat, and was worth over a billion dollars.

Tuck jogged through the basement, past the theater, entertainment room, and indoor pool. He tried to sneak up the stairs so she couldn't hear him coming and investigate. Hurrying through the foyer so he could ascend to the third floor which only housed his rooms, he couldn't resist peeking into the study. A small woman with a cascade of blonde curls stood next to his bookshelf with a Baldacci novel in hand. Hmm. He couldn't see her face clearly, but someone who was interested in Baldacci couldn't be too bad, could they?

Chapter Two

Mr. Braxton returned with a tray of tea, coffee, and pastries. Maryn had lost herself for a few minutes in *The Last Mile* by David Baldacci. She loved that book. Now her stomach was churning too much to eat anything. Where was this guy? She'd been here for over fifteen minutes and was beginning to wonder if he planned on speaking to her at all. Typical rich jerk, thought everyone was just waiting around for him all day.

She shook out her hands and focused on snapping a few pictures of the office. If only Mr. Shaffer had allowed a camera crew to accompany her. Her paltry skills at photography would have to do.

"My apologies, ma'am. Mr. Shaffer will be joining us shortly."

"You sure about that?"

He cleared his throat. "Um, yes, ma'am. Can I offer you some tea?"

She hid a smile. This guy had missed his era and continent. He should've lived in eighteenth century England.

"No, thank you. Water would be heavenly though."

"But of course. Sparkling, bottled, or tap?"

"Is the tap good?" Being raised in Southern California, she'd hated the tap water and remembered begging her mom to put flavor in hers. Now she drank bottled.

"It is lovely, ma'am, straight out of a mountain spring."

"Oh? Tap sounds fabulous." She'd never had water from a real mountain spring, only the promises of one from The Fresh Water Man.

He left and she drummed her fingers on her jeans then stood and paced. Mr. Braxton returned with a glass of ice water. Maryn took a long drink and grinned at him. "Best water I've ever had."

"Thank you, ma'am. Can I interest you in a novel to read while you wait?"

"Be straight with me. Is he coming?"

Mr. Braxton pressed his lips together. "I assure you he is."

"Is he ditching me?"

Mr. Braxton's face reddened. "No, ma'am, he's just... freshening up."

Maryn tilted her head to the side. Tucker Shaffer cared to freshen up for her. That didn't fit his persona. "Why?"

"You arrived a bit earlier than anticipated and he was..." Mr. Braxton's mouth twisted then he spit out the word, "Sweaty."

Maryn laughed. She always tried to be a few minutes early to appointments rather than late. "I don't mind sweaty." In fact, she fully appreciated a man who was willing to sweat.

"You would've minded this," a deep voice rumbled from behind her.

Maryn whirled around to get her first look at Tucker Shaffer. My, oh, my. The man must've sweated on more than one occasion to get a build like that. Dressed in an untucked button-down shirt and jeans, he was over six feet tall with broad shoulders, a thick waist, and legs like tree trunks. She doubted anyone would dare call him overweight, but he was definitely... well-built. His dark hair was long, almost to his chin, and curled slightly. His mouth was a great shape with a bowed upper lip and full lower one and his face was that hard-working kind of handsome, the type that spent a lot of time outdoors but was still almost too good-looking. His eyes really drew her in. They were dark brown and expressive. Those eyes had stories to tell and she planned to hear them. She knew this was the interview that would guarantee her a successful career and as long as he didn't pick her up and toss her out of here, she was definitely overstaying her welcome today.

Maryn grinned at him and took a step forward with her hand outstretched. "Mr. Shaffer?"

"Tucker," his voice was almost a growl, like he didn't use it very often. He walked across the room and engulfed her smaller hand with his. Maryn wondered if she'd ever liked a handshake as much as she liked this one. He cleared his throat and his voice was clearer this time, but still deep enough that a little thrill of pleasure rushed through her. "You're Ms. Howe?"

"Maryn to you." She gave him a saucy wink.

He smiled and the effect was dynamic. No wonder he was an overnight success. She itched to take a picture, but didn't want to tick him off in the first five minutes.

Tucker released her hand and gestured to the comfortable chairs by the fire. Maryn sank into the soft leather. He sat kitty-corner to her. "Would you like something different to drink?"

Maryn shook her head. "I have this delicious water."

"Brax, a Dr. Pepper, please."

"Yes, sir."

Maryn could swear that was a sarcastic "sir". His help was interesting, to say the least.

Tucker grinned roguishly at the man. Mr. Braxton shook his head slightly and strode from the room.

Maryn focused on this enigmatic man next to her. Why was he

a hermit? Everything about him screamed charisma and he was definitely handsome enough and wealthy enough to have scores of women begging for attention. She knew she'd beg if she wasn't so prideful and wasn't sort of dating James. Ah, James would have to forgive her, if Tucker Shaffer showed the slightest bit of interest, she'd be a goner. It wasn't like she'd committed to date James exclusively.

"Thank you for gracing me with your presence." That had come out kind of bratty. "I mean, I'm ecstatic to be here and be allowed to interview you. It's a pleasure."

"Wasn't really my idea." He studied his large hands as he spoke.

"Whose idea was it?"

"PR." He gave her a tilted smile that revealed a small scar in the corner of his lip. Maryn clasped her hands in her lap to resist touching that scar. Actors would replicate that sexy look and no one would blame them. Holy moly, she needed to focus.

"My PR team is a pain in the butt," he said.

A loud chortle came out before Maryn clamped her hand to her lips. "I know how that is, my editor is the same."

Mr. Braxton brought Tucker's soda.

"Thanks, Brax."

Maryn noticed the familiarity. These two were playing a part, she was sure of it.

"Sir." Mr. Braxton quickly left the room.

Tucker sipped from the can, set it on a side table, then spread his hands wide. "So, Maryn, interview away."

Maryn couldn't remember a single question she had. All she could think about was the size of those hands and secretly wish they were holding hers still. She pulled out her phone, grateful for notes and opened the app. Sadly, before she could ask any of the

14

reasonable, well-thought out questions she'd agonized over, it popped out, "Why are you such a recluse?"

Tucker pumped his eyebrows and grinned at her. "If you had a place like this, would you want to go deal with society?"

She recognized deflection when she heard it. No matter. She'd get to the grit before the sun set and she needed to go check into The Angler's Lodge. Tomorrow she'd have to wake up early to drive the two hours to Idaho Falls and make her return flight, but she was going to enjoy today. "This is a fabulous house. Can you give me a tour?"

"Sure." Tucker stood.

Maryn rose next to him. Even with two inches on her boots, she only came to his chin. Curse being short. Tucker probably liked tall models to compliment his large stature. Not that it mattered—she was here for an exclusive interview, nothing more. She'd better remind herself of that every few minutes.

As they walked, she thought to ask one of her questions and found that she really wanted to know the answer, "What do you do to keep busy? Give me a typical day in the life of Tucker Shaffer."

"Everyone probably assumes I sit around doing nothing all day."

"If they assume that they obviously haven't seen how built you are."

He chuckled and directed her into the great room. Maryn got distracted for a minute gushing over the view and then all the different wood work. From the fireplace mantle to the wood encasing the windows to the gorgeous cabinetry, she was smitten by this house. "Let me just stand here by this beautiful fireplace for a minute and thaw out," she said. "Why's it so cold up here? It's October third for heaven's sake."

Tucker glanced down at her with a smirk. "It's snowed in September before."

Maryn shivered and moved closer to the fire and to him. "Okay, answer my question then we'll finish the tour."

Tucker rubbed his large palms together and studied the flames in the gas fireplace. "I try to balance my days—exercise, work around the house and yard, business, and programming."

She tilted her head to the side. "I've heard some tales about all the time you spend doing volunteer work. You like to fix things and teach people how to work, in addition to donating large sums of money."

"You really do your research, don't you?"

Maryn looked up and down his large frame. "You have no idea."

He blushed and she absolutely loved it. He had no clue how good-looking and powerful he was. He was so different from the wealthy men she'd met who thought they owned the world, the powerful men who thought they owned everyone in the world, and the good-looking men who thought they should own her and every other woman.

"So, for exercise, you like to..."

"Run, lift weights, box, and I get a lot of movement working outside, driving my gardeners crazy."

"Nice. I loved the gardener at the estate my mother worked on. He was so patient with me and always let me pick the flowers..." She trailed off as he listened to her like it was the most important thing he had to do today. "The programming?"

He swallowed and gave her a kind smile, not commenting on her revelation that she'd been the hired help. She was so beneath him socially it wasn't even funny. If you cared about social ladders, which she didn't.

"Everyone assumes after I designed Friend Zone I was done, but I've created a lot of other games and apps. I just market them under different names."

"Why?"

He spread his hands and smirked at her. "Avoid taxes, why else?"

She laughed. "Okay, I'll buy that. Whose names?"

"Whoever I want to share the money with—usually Mama Porter, Johnson, and Brax." He shrugged like it was no big deal.

Maryn's eyes widened. "That's pretty impressive, Tucker Shaffer. Hey. Are you just trying to impress me?"

He smiled at her. "I don't know, is it working?"

"So far it is." The warmth of the fire and the warmth of his gaze both made her a bit flushed. "Okay. I'm ready to finish the tour, then I want to sit by this fireplace and grill you some more."

Tucker blew out a long breath. "Don't you have enough information already?"

Maryn laughed. "Yeah, I'm going to print a premier article and all I've got is how you spend your days and how good-looking you are."

Tucker grinned at that and the scar in the corner of his lips was tempting her. She wanted to know how he got it, after she kissed it, that is. Whoa, she needed to focus. "Sorry," she explained. "My mouth tends to run too much."

"No, you're great. I feel very... comfortable with you."

Maryn grinned.

"But I don't like my life being on display. I'm not sure why I let them talk me into this."

"Come on, big guy, has it been that hard on you?"

He chuckled at that. "Not so far, but you know what they say about beautiful reporters?"

Maryn bit at her lip to hide a smile. "No, what's that?"

"They could talk a saint into hell."

"Oh, that's awful. I have no desire to talk anyone into that place. I'm going to heaven to be with my Granny Ellie, thank you very much." Maryn pressed her lips together. She had to stop revealing too much. Be professional, she reminded herself.

Tucker placed a hand on her back and directed her toward the front staircase again. She loved the warmth of his large palm on her back. "I'm sorry about your Granny Ellie."

"She's actually not mine, but my best friend's. Granny Ellie just adopted me and I miss her. She was the one person who always appreciated my snide comments."

Tucker looked sharply at her. "You don't have family of your own?"

"No one to brag about. I have my mom. She tried. Worked her butt off in more ways than one so I could have some sort of life." *Family of her own?* In her childish dreams.

"I'm sorry to hear that."

"No, no, no, we aren't here to talk about me." Maryn mentally shook herself. Why was she opening up to this guy? She needed her head examined. Yes, she tended to talk too much and use funny expressions, but she usually employed those techniques to put people at ease, not tell her life story. It had taken James two years to know as much about her as she'd revealed to Tucker in twenty minutes. Cripes! "Tell me more about your volunteer work. Is it always local?"

Tucker gave her an appraising look, but told her a little about his latest humanitarian trip to Ethiopia where they'd been able to dig safer wells and help some villages plant community gardens. Maryn was more and more impressed with this man. Today was looking to be one of the most interesting and productive of her career and the man at her side was looking to be a dream come true, for a reporter with good interview skills that is. Not for a woman who already had a sort of boyfriend.

Tuck had to resist touching the beautiful Maryn as they sauntered through his house. She oohed and aahed over the woodwork, the huge windows showcasing the forest and the river beyond, and the decorations that were rustic and comfortable. He'd never been around such a small person with so much energy. He liked her bold manner of speaking and he loved the way her face lit up as she talked. When he met her gaze and those blue eyes sparkled, he talked himself into believing the sparkle was just for him.

They'd finished the tour and were lounging in the enclosed, heated patio off the back of his great room. Mama Porter bustled out of the kitchen with a tray of steaming food. Tuck stood quickly and took the tray from her. "You don't need to serve us," he said.

"Of course I do. We've got a guest." She beamed at Maryn. "And she's such a beauty. Hello, love, I'm Mama Porter. It's wonderful to have you here."

Maryn stood and held out her hand. Mama Porter placed it between her plump fingers.

"Thank you. This smells exquisite. I'm Maryn."

"Oh, I know who you are. Have you got all the information you need for your article, my dear?" Mama Porter released Maryn's hand, gestured for her to sit, and started uncovering platters of orange chicken, ham-fried rice, and chow mein.

"No, actually." Maryn cocked her head to the side and pinned him with a stare. "Tucker is very skilled at evading some of the questions I need answered and getting information out of me that I don't usually share."

Tucker rubbed at his suddenly warm neck. Maryn was a professional and she'd come to get an exclusive interview. Of course she wouldn't be happy to have pictures of his house and a little bit of inside information about the different products he'd created and his latest humanitarian trip.

He'd tried all afternoon to get to know her better, but all he really obtained was she was born and raised in southern California, with her mother, but her best friend, Alyssa, and adopted Granny were her real family. She didn't surf because her best friend had a deformed foot so they'd never tried surfing, but she loved to swim in the ocean.

Mama Porter darted a gaze at him. She knew how much he appreciated his privacy, but she'd been with him for five years now and treated him like one of the sons she'd lost. "I wish I could reveal all his secrets dear, but that's not my place."

Tucker heard a low growl escape from his throat. He clamped his lips to keep it in.

Mama Porter gave him a warning look as Maryn eyed him with concern. Why didn't she jump and run away? Most women would probably be terrified of how big and unwelcoming he was. He smiled to himself. Maryn made it impossible to not be welcoming as she teased him and made him smile.

"I hope you enjoy Chinese food," Mama Porter said.

"I love it." Maryn grinned. "Thank you for dinner. I'm sure it will be delicious."

Mama Porter scurried away.

"Won't you be joining us?" Maryn asked before the patio door closed and sealed them alone again. There was a little trepidation in her voice. She *was* scared of him and who could blame her? A teeny little thing and he probably looked like an ogre with his huge body. He was evil, but she couldn't know that. No one but his closest friends knew and would ever know.

"No, dear." Mama Porter poked her head through the door. "I'll give you that chance to get him to open up."

Tucker glared at her, but she simply blew him a kiss and banged into the house. An awkward silence followed. Tucker offered Maryn the fried rice first, dishing up his plate with each dish after she'd taken what she wanted. He was pleasantly surprised that she took a decent serving size and actually started eating. The few young women he'd tried to date when he first made his money had claimed to never be hungry. He didn't understand how someone couldn't be hungry as he loved to eat almost as much as he loved to be left alone.

"So..." Maryn set down her fork and faced him bravely. "Are you going to answer any of my questions?"

"I've answered... some of them." He pushed noodles around on his plate. The fear of her discovering his secrets closed his throat and made him feel claustrophobic, like he was still hiding in a cave in Afghanistan with nothing but his pistol, semi-automatic rifle, and Johnson as protection. He took a swallow of water. "What would you like to know?"

"First of all, why are you a recluse?"

"You're some big time writer and the burning question is the same one that everyone asks me?" He bit at his cheek. He was being too harsh.

Maryn arched her delicate eyebrows and waited.

Pushing some food around on his plate, he finally muttered, "Honestly, it's just the same old story."

"Which is?"

He met her gaze and found himself falling into those blue eyes. He stuttered out the response his PR people had drilled into him, "I made my money fast and I didn't know who to trust. I surround myself with a few people who have been true to me and I stay away from the rest."

"You're right, that is a lame old story." Maryn smiled to soften her words. "Would you ever tell *me* the truth?"

Tuck blinked at her. If she kept smiling at him like that, he'd tell her a lot of things that he shouldn't. "That is the truth... okay, some of the truth."

"Did a woman break your heart?"

Tuck chuckled and forked a bite of orange chicken. "Never been close enough to a woman to allow that to happen."

"Interesting. The famous Tucker Shaffer doesn't like women?"

The orange chicken caught in his throat. He swallowed and shook his head. "I definitely *like* women." *Especially feisty blondes.* "I just haven't had an opportunity to meet the right one."

Maryn glanced outside then back at him. Her blue eyes pierced right through him and Tuck wondered what he could do to get her to stay here, with him. No. That was crazy thinking. A gorgeous, city-born woman would never be happy with his lifestyle.

"Kind of hard to find that opportunity with a guard who's a stiff, a butler who's stuck in the eighteenth century, and a cook who reminds me of Mrs. Potts from Beauty and the Beast."

"You can be Beauty and I'll be the Beast," the words were out before Tuck could stop them.

Maryn's eyes widened, but then a small smile curled her lips. "I've had worse offers."

Tuck loved the way she talked, but sometimes wasn't sure what she meant. She'd had worse offers, but had she had better? He'd checked and there was no wedding ring, but that didn't mean there was no boyfriend. Oh, he was pathetic. The first woman he truly interacted with in the past six months and he was drooling over her like a teenage boy.

"You were raised in foster care," Maryn said. "Do you keep in touch with any of your families?"

Tuck's chest tightened. They'd moved from what he would consider flirtation to his awkward childhood. Fabulous. "Only Brax."

"Mr. Braxton was one of your foster fathers?"

"Grandfather. I lived with his daughter and her family from ten to twelve years old. Brax and I had a connection and kept in touch for years. He encouraged me and believed in me when no one else did. When I had my success, it was about the same time that he was retiring from being a doctor, and his wife had passed away a few years before that, so I talked him into staying with me. He's amazing with investments and the business side of things." That was a long speech, hopefully it would satisfy her reporter curiosity.

"He's not really your butler."

"No." Tuck smiled and shook his head. "When Johnson first met him he teased that Brax was stiff and proper like an English butler. They have a bet going when we have guests. Guess Brax won this time."

"There's a story behind all of your staff, isn't there?"

"All three of them?"

"Three?" Her eyes widened and she glanced around. "Only three? How do you maintain all the property you have with a staff of three?"

He shrugged. "I pay caretakers when I'm not at one of my homes. When we're living there we have a maid service come in twice a week and keep a gardener on staff, but all of us pitch in to upkeep the house and yard of wherever we live."

"So the stiff outside isn't really a guard dog?"

Tuck laughed so hard his side hurt. He never laughed like that. "Maybe Johnson won the bet with Brax after all. He's a buddy from college. He enrolled in the Army to put himself through school, was deployed to Afghanistan for eighteen months." He clenched his fist, not sure why he was revealing all of this. He cleared his throat and looked down, lest she see the truth in his eyes. "He saw and was commanded to do some things that scarred him pretty good. He likes to patrol the property and watch the cameras, but only uses his weapons now to hunt and pretend to be a guard when people stop by. He's brilliant with real estate and takes care of all of those kinds of transactions for us. He's also more social than the rest of us and gets out and makes friends wherever we live." No reason to tell her the things he and Johnson had seen together.

"Does sweet Mama Porter cook *and* clean?"

"I do a lot of the day to day stuff and everyone pitches in, then like I said I have a cleaning service come in twice a week and scour the place."

Maryn took a slow breath. "You're not what I expected, Tucker Shaffer."

"Is anyone ever what you expect?" Tuck wondered if she liked what she learned about him or liked her original perception of him more.

"Good point. So, tell me more."

He laughed and shook his head. No way was she getting much more out of him than she'd already gotten. Unless she was willing to go on a date with him sometime soon. "I've already told you more than any reporter I've ever met."

"That wasn't tough, you've never talked to any reporters."

"Good thing I liked you the first time I saw you or I would've thrown you out."

"Would you really?"

Tuck had to look down. He folded his napkin and placed it on his near-empty plate. "Probably."

"Why do you want people to be afraid of you?"

Tuck hunched over, feeling like she'd punched him in the gut. "It's just easier that way."

"So the mysterious, ultra-wealthy loner who frightens everyone away is really a softy who cleans toilets and only allows those he's trusted for years close to him." She leaned toward him and he smelled a fresh, clean scent. It reminded him of sunshine and lilacs.

Tuck lifted his hands. "I don't clean toilets."

She smiled. "Why keep the world at arm's length?"

"How much of this are you going to print? You aren't writing anything down."

She tapped her head. "Near perfect memory. At least when I care about what I'm learning. I promise I'll send you the article before it goes to print for your approval."

"I really don't want all my secrets out to the world." His voice dropped and he should've been embarrassed as he said, "If you were asking for Maryn Howe instead of for *The Rising Star*, I might be persuaded to reveal a secret or two."

She tilted her head to the side. That silky blonde hair trailed over her shoulder and Tuck wanted more than anything to entwine his fingers in it.

"Are we that friendly?" she asked.

Tuck suddenly realized what a fool he was, coming onto the reporter who only wanted any dirt he was willing to reveal. He needed to get a social life. Maybe he could find a nice girl at the local church they attended on Sundays or let Johnson set him up. Tuck hadn't dated much the past few years, but obviously it was time if he could feel an immediate connection and attraction to someone who needed to be kept farther than arm's length.

"Why didn't you show me the third floor?" Maryn asked.

Tuck drew in a slow breath. "That's my private suite. I don't show it to anyone, most of all to reporters."

"What if I was asking as Maryn Howe not as *The Rising Star?* I promise not to take any pictures or print anything you tell me on that floor."

Tuck knew he was a lonely, depraved idiot, but it wasn't like she was going to open drawers, look through his desk, or find everything he wanted to hide. He stood, offered her his hand, and said, "Okay."

Maryn tried not to stare at Tucker as they ascended the grand staircase then kept winding up and up. Glancing out the windows, she could see snow swirling in the air. She sucked in a breath. "Look at that! It's so pretty. I've never seen snow before."

"Really?"

"California girl."

He grinned at her. Maryn smiled back, but then suddenly realized she'd have to drive in this snow. How terrifying, but she couldn't leave now, she was just getting to the good stuff with Tucker. No way was a little white fluff going to interrupt that. She'd just have to be extra careful and pray the snow stopped.

The Feisty One

Tucker rested his hand on her back, but when she glanced up, he quickly dropped it. He was... prickly and handsome and he just had presence. Definitely more interesting than any man she'd ever encountered. His eyes were so full of secrets she felt like she was wading through half-truths every time he told her something. What was he hiding? He'd been in the Army with Johnson; she knew that from her research. Why lie and say that only Johnson had scars from service? What had he done in Afghanistan that had affected him so deeply? If only she could snoop a little more. Instant guilt arose. Tucker had been very kind and accommodating to her. He didn't deserve his dirt displayed for the world to mock. Whatever she discovered by the time she left here today, she vowed to paint him in a good light.

Tucker opened the double doors and Maryn's jaw dropped open. They entered a sitting area first with floor to ceiling windows. Fat snowflakes floated from the sky. She should say her goodbyes and find her hotel before the roads got too dangerous, but she couldn't force herself to leave yet. There was still much more to learn about Tucker and she wanted to be the one to learn it. Oddly enough, the article was no longer the number one reason for spending more time with him.

The walls of the room were knotty pine and all the furnishings were a deep reddish-brown leather, except for a mahogany desk and a cherry wood mantle over the granite-surround of the fireplace. There was an archway to her right into a bedroom with a massive bed and she could see an arched bathroom entrance and a walk-in closet beyond that.

"This is amazing," Maryn breathed.

Tucker's face relaxed into a smile. "Thank you. My private sanctuary."

"Thank you for sharing it with me. I won't... take any pictures or write about it." Their eyes met and held and she whispered, "I promise." Many wealthy people had private rooms they didn't want on display, but there was something more here, she felt it. She would keep her promise, even from James and Alyssa. Thinking of James made her feel guilty. He wouldn't appreciate the way she was so intrigued by this man. She needed to keep this attraction under control, but when Tucker nodded his thanks and gave her a brief smile, darn if that scar next to his lip didn't appear. Thoughts of James were pushed far away.

Tucker gestured toward the overstuffed leather seats by the gas fireplace. A quick click of a button on the remote and the fire sprang to life. Maryn sank down and studied the churning snowstorm outside. It was truly beautiful. "This is perfect. If only I didn't have to drive in the snow and could sit here with a cup of cocoa and a Baldacci novel."

"I think you're going to get your wish. These snowstorms can be vicious. You'll have to stay until it passes."

The muscles in Maryn's neck tightened. She'd wanted that invite and she definitely didn't want to drive in the snow, but what if things became awkward? "Oh, I couldn't possibly... stay."

She felt his gaze on her and almost gasped at the amused and honestly wicked glint in his brown eyes.

"I've had enough bad press." Tucker spread his hands, the picture of innocence, except for the searing look in those eyes. "I'm not going to add, 'threw a reporter out of his house in a blizzard where she slid off the road and received gaping wounds then caught hypothermia and died,' to the stack."

Maryn took a long breath. Her gaze returned to the lodge pole pines being loaded with snow. Whereas the view used to include the

28

river, it was now impossible to see past the first row of trees. She'd never experienced snow, but would assume this was what the newscasters meant when they said a whiteout. The storm had come on quick.

"I don't want to impose," she murmured.

"Mama Porter would be thrilled," he said.

"What about you?" she asked before she could stop herself, curse her errant tongue.

"I would be... grateful for the opportunity."

"Opportunity to do what?"

"Get to know my beautiful reporter better."

"And here everyone claims you have no social skills."

Tucker's eyes darkened but his smile remained in place. "If you stay, you'll be able to tell them a different story."

Goosebumps rose on Maryn's arms. She wasn't sure what story she was going to tell when this adventure was over, but the idea of spending more time with him had every nerve singing. She licked her lips and then forced herself to focus on the beautiful scenery outside, lest he notice her drooling over him.

Tucker's phone rang. "Excuse me," he said, standing and walking into his bedroom.

Maryn also stood and walked around, looking at the artwork he'd chosen to display. She was shocked to see one of her friend, Alyssa's, photographs on the wall. This man liked Baldacci novels and A.A.'s photography. Of course, Alyssa was now married to Beckham Taylor, but she still did her artwork under A.A. Maryn was beginning to think that Tucker was too good to be true. Why had everyone made him out to be a social cipher and a jerk?

Tucker was still talking in the other room, something about a grizzly bear on the property which had entered through the river. It sounded like the guard dog, Johnson, was monitoring the situation. She shivered. She'd never seen a bear except for at the zoo, but they still gave her nightmares. Taking Tucker up on his offer to stay inside this safe, beautiful house sounded better and better.

She paused at an antique roll top desk nestled against one wall. She wanted to open it in the worst way. Curse reporter instincts. She'd promised Tucker she wouldn't reveal anything she learned in his rooms, so what would it hurt to look?

Unable to resist, she made sure Tucker wasn't looking, and slowly lifted the cover. Photos were scattered over the desk, all of them snapshots of beautiful children near a cave entrance. The scenery was brown, possibly desert. They appeared to be of Arab descent. Maryn wondered what the connection was to Tucker. She picked up a picture of a darling boy, who couldn't have been more than eight or nine. Turning the print over, she read, "Murdered by Lieutenant Tucker Shaffer."

She gasped and dropped the picture like it was a hot ember from the fire. Her heart thumped louder and louder. Had she really seen that? It couldn't be true. Tucker seemed like such a nice guy.

Leaning back, she spied Tucker inclining against the four-poster bed with the phone to his ear. Maryn picked up a snapshot of a teenage girl with flowing black hair and a beautiful smile. She slowly turned it over and the same words were written in bold marker, "Murdered by Lieutenant Tucker Shaffer." Her eyes darted over the pictures, ice rubbing along her spine. There were at least half a dozen of the pictures. He couldn't possibly have... killed all these children?

Cold fear pricked at her neck. She needed to get out of this house. "Okay, girl," she muttered to herself, "play it cool and then make a quick exit. He'll never know."

Setting the picture down, she grabbed the top and started rolling it down. It squeaked. She gasped and moved it slower, saying a quick prayer for help. She noticed the silence a split second before she could feel his breath on her cheek.

"Did you find what you were looking for?" he asked, his voice a low growl.

Maryn released the desktop, whipped around to face him, and tried to back up, but she was pressed into the desk. "I'm sorry. I didn't mean to see. I was just looking around. They were sitting right on your desk." She hated that her voice squeaked but her throat was closing off.

He leaned into her space, his dark eyes snapping. "Did you find what you were looking for?" he repeated.

"I-I think I need to go."

"Screw the bad publicity," he snarled. "You think I'm going to let you leave now? Tell the whole world about what a monster Tucker Shaffer really is?" His lips curled into a feral grin. His brown eyes had turned black and cold.

Maryn's breath was coming in short bursts. He wasn't touching her, but she felt like she was standing in the shadow of a calculating animal and he was going to lash out at any second. Being mugged last summer was less terrifying than the look in Tucker Shaffer's eyes. How had the warm, friendly man morphed into this beast?

Without thinking, she stomped on his foot with the heel of her red boots. He cried out, probably more in surprise than pain. She ducked under his arm and sprinted out the door. She ran down the three flights of steps without looking back to see if he pursued. Mr. Braxton was in the office and glanced up in surprise when she yanked the front door open.

"Ms. Howe?" He hurried into the foyer. "Where are you going? There's a bear and—"

"I'll take my chances," she muttered, flying down the front steps and ignoring whatever else Mr. Braxton was trying to say. Her little red rental car was still sitting there in the circle. At least they hadn't moved her car and kept her prisoner. There was something very wrong with this house and the people inside.

Maryn slipped on the snow and went down hard. Her elbow and knee slammed onto the wet pavement. She hauled herself up, limping and sliding the remaining steps to her car, these cute boots were not made for snow. She peered through the thick snow, waiting for a grizzly bear to rip her apart. Not sure if she was more scared of a real grizzly bear out in this forest, or the beast of a man inside the house. She chanced a glance up, up to the third story. Tucker Shaffer stood at the window. Thank heavens she couldn't distinguish his expression through the snowstorm, and double thank heavens he wasn't chasing after her.

Yanking her door open, she stumbled into her car and hit the lock button. The trees and falling snow all gave the illusion of peace, looking like a stinking Christmas card. Maryn shuddered. There was no peace in this place and the sooner she got out of here the better. Her hand shook as she pulled the keys from her pocket and started the car. She put the car in gear, pressed the gas pedal too far to the floor, and squealed down the driveway.

She could barely see through the thick flakes covering the windshield and her wipers had no hope of doing their job. Something flashed through the trees to her right. It couldn't be the bear, could it? She shuddered, the sooner she got out of Satan's lair the better.

Her terror had her gripping the steering wheel and coaxing the car into faster speeds. Rental cars out of Idaho Falls had to have good tires, right? They had snow in that place six months out of the year. Greatest snow on earth and all that bunk or... wait, was that Utah? It didn't matter. All she had to do was keep the car on this nice asphalt driveway and then hopefully get through the gate. What if the gate was locked and didn't open automatically? Oh, heavens. It had looked pretty strong. Could she ram it? She shook her head. If she couldn't get through the gate, she'd climb it and run down the main road until someone came along to help her. She could call the police and get some help. Duh! The police. She pulled her phone out of her pocket.

A deer came out of nowhere. Maryn screamed. She yanked the steering wheel to the left with slick hands. Panic clawed at her throat as the deer stared into her headlights with his huge eyes. *Please don't let me kill him,* she prayed.

Her car squealed off the road and Maryn's stomach dropped as it cruised down a slight embankment. A tree loomed in front of her. "No," she cried out, trying to correct, but it was too late. The tree smacked the front of her car with a loud bang. The seatbelt caught her, yanking at her chest then the airbag slammed her back against the seat.

Coughing out the dust, Maryn sat stunned for a minute. She tried to beat the airbag out of her way and it slowly deflated. Reaching around and jamming the gearshift into reverse, she pressed down on the gas pedal, but sadly the wheels just spun and squealed in protest. She gunned it from drive to reverse for several minutes with equally frustrating results. This was not good.

Where was that dang phone? She must've dropped it when the airbag blasted into her. Pushing the annoying balloon of plastic out of the way, she groped with her fingers along the floor until she finally connected with slick metal and held it up.

Please, let me be able to get some help. No service. Not even one blasted bar. She sighed with disgust. Just what she needed. She'd only had one bar as she drove into this cursed place and the storm was probably wiping out any signal. Dropping the phone back into her jacket pocket, she evaluated her options. Stay and wait for Tucker to find her, stay and wait for a bear to eat her, or be a tough woman and hike her butt out of this nightmare?

The snow had already covered her car. She couldn't even look outside and see if the bear, Tucker Shaffer, or the guard dog were hunting her down. She shivered and turned on the windshield wipers, feeling marginally better when she could at least look at the tree that had squished her rental car.

She had to be close to the gate. No matter how cold and wet it was outside, she wasn't parking her tush here any longer. The bear was supposedly on the property and she was like a sitting duck in this wrecked car. Plus, there was no way she was facing Tucker again. If she could get through the gate, she'd be rescued. She would flag someone down on the main road and be safe at her hotel within an hour. Soon she'd be drinking hot cocoa, talking to Alyssa on the phone, and laughing about how crazy this all was.

What would she tell Alyssa and James about all of this insanity? Remembering the great impression she'd originally had of Tucker made her wonder if she would include anything about those photos and his psycho-man reaction in her article. She'd promised him she wouldn't share anything about the third floor, and she always kept her promises, but that was before he went crazy on her. She shook her head. Who cared about the stupid article right now? All she wanted was to get away from this snowy purgatory.

Gingerly opening the door, she swung her head around and listened for a minute. It was deceitfully calm as the thick snow covered any sound and wiped out all visibility. Sliding out from under the airbag, she evaluated her injuries. Her elbow and knee were both aching from the fall in the driveway, but besides knocking the air out of her and probably bruising her chest, the seatbelt and airbag had done their jobs.

She hugged herself for warmth and cursed her thin jacket and high-heeled boots as she started down the pavement that should lead to the gate and escape. The road twisted and turned. She started to wonder if she'd taken a wrong path. There had been numerous paved paths leading off the main one when she drove through this afternoon. In this thick snow, she couldn't see the asphalt, covered with inches of snow, except where her boots left a thin trail.

She had to be on the right path. Any other option could mean death. Death. The closest she'd ever come to that terrifying word was being mugged last summer, but all the punk had really wanted was some cash to buy alcohol. He'd barely roughed her up and though he'd threatened to hurt her, as soon as she gave him money, he'd taken off. Why had she ever left the city? A mugging was nothing compared to this.

Her gaze darted around the thick snow and even thicker trees. A shiver raced through her that had nothing to do with the fact that she couldn't feel her toes. If she didn't get out of here soon, she'd freeze or a bear would rip her to shreds. Suddenly, Tucker Shaffer's house of crazies didn't sound so bad.

Chapter Three

"What happened?" Mama Porter's voice was as soft as the hand on his shoulder.

Tuck concentrated on the red car peeling out of his driveway. "She saw..." He shook his head and gestured to the desk, cursing himself for not hiding or burning those pictures. "And I behaved badly." That was a huge understatement. Why didn't he control his temper? All the old fears and insecurities had arisen, but most of all was the worry of what she thought of him. Instead of trying to fix the situation, he'd turned into a growling jerk.

"Why didn't you explain?"

Tuck gave a self-deprecating laugh. "Explain what? That I killed those children? That would surely make everything better."

"You talk yourself into being a monster, but you're not." Mama Porter gently patted his shoulder and then left. There wasn't anything she or anyone else could say.

Tuck raised his head and watched the snow fall from the heavens. He shouldn't have let Maryn go out in this, but she was probably safer in the elements than in the house with him. He buried his head in his hands and wallowed in self-pity. His PR people were going to be so ticked at him, but he didn't really care. He was too upset at himself for terrifying Maryn. He'd started to believe they had a chance to become friends at least. What could he have done differently? Besides keeping her out of his rooms. He couldn't have explained. There was no excuse for what he'd done that day and the fear in her eyes would've only grown. That fear had ripped at his insides. He shook his head and cursed again.

His phone rang. He didn't answer it. It rang again and again. Finally, he swiped the screen open and barked, "What?"

"I've lost track of the bear in this storm," Johnson informed him.

A clutch of fear hit him. What if Maryn encountered that bear? She'd be safe, as long as she stayed in the car. "Johnson, Maryn left. Did you get her out of the gate?"

"That's the other problem. When I got back to the gatehouse, there was no sign that she had left. I backtracked and found her car. Looks like she hit a tree, but... she isn't in the car."

Tucker jumped to his feet, grabbed a sweatshirt off a chair, and ran down the stairs. "Find her," he ordered Johnson.

He headed all the way to the basement and unlocked his safe, grabbing a .33 caliber big bore rifle. Sprinting to his lower garage, he jumped onto a four-wheeler and yelled at Braxton, who had followed him, "Call the sheriff. Get Search and Rescue on their way. Maryn's out in the storm and there's a grizzly on the loose."

He peeled out of the garage and wished he hadn't heard Braxton's words, "She'll be dead before the sheriff gets here."

Chapter Four

Maryn hated cold. Her feet and hands were so numb she wasn't sure they were part of her body anymore. She couldn't stop shivering as her temperature seemed to drop more with each second. Even her face hurt, every flake stinging like a bee sting. Snow was not pretty anymore. It was evil.

When she got home to California, she would refuse any assignment that wasn't on a tropical island. She shoved her hands into the pockets of her waste of material, stylish jacket and plunged on. That stupid gate should be in sight, any time now. She started begging the Lord to help her out of this situation.

The fence appeared next to the road. No, no, no! She couldn't have gotten lost. This should be the gate. How had she not noticed that she'd veered off the main road? Fear clawed at her throat, tasting metallic. How was she going to get out of here? She'd have to stay next to the fence and hope she was going toward the gate, not circling back to the mansion of scary guy. Actually, she'd take her chances with him right now.

Could she climb the fence? She looked up. It was wrought iron, straight up, with spiky bars at the top. She didn't hear a hum so it probably wasn't electric, but who knew what kind of newfangled contraption Tucker Shaffer might be capable of.

She ripped a pine cone off a nearby tree and chucked it at the fence. It bounced off without bursting into flames or getting zapped by blue lightning. Wrapping her stiff hands around the cold iron, she tried to scramble up. The slick metal seemed to laugh at her as she slid right back to the ground. Crap. Her hands ached like she was a ninety-year old with arthritis. She forced herself to try again, but couldn't get her fingers to even grip the metal. She rubbed her fingers together to bring back some circulation but it didn't help. No hope but to find that stupid gate.

An uneven thumping sound came from behind her. Maryn searched the whiteness. The sun had gone down shortly after she started walking and the approaching night didn't give much reassurance of any kind of visibility with this blasted snowstorm. She couldn't see anything, but the hair on the back of her neck stood up as she heard breathing.

No. She was imagining things. It wasn't a bear. It wasn't Tucker Shaffer. Though at this point she'd take Tucker over the bear. A man could at least be reasoned with, right? Maybe. He'd been pretty terrifying.

Just hold onto the fence and keep walking. Maryn started pleading with a merciful Father in Heaven to please, please get her out of this mess. She started making all kinds of bargains—she'd call her mother every week and she'd settle down and marry James, even though she didn't really love him, but it would make him happy and since she was going to dedicate her life to service as soon as she was safe and warm, marrying James was a good first step. Then they'd both give up writing articles about celebrities and go to work for Beckham and Alyssa and their charity stuff. James would hate that, but she was making a sacrifice to marry him so he could make sacrifices too.

The thumping and the breathing were growing louder and louder. Maryn wanted to sob. The hand brushing a new bar every few seconds was stiff and shaking terribly. She couldn't hold on any longer. It was all she could do to simply drag her frozen fingers along the metal so she wouldn't get lost. Her feet were just blocks of ice at the end of her legs. Shaking so hard, her teeth were knocking together, she couldn't see anything past the cold. Even her eyelashes were frozen and heavy. Trying to blink, she could barely see past the ice coating her lashes.

She stumbled over a log or something and went down to her knees. Wet snow seeped through her pants. More cold. Insult to injury, but still she wanted to stay on the ground and bawl. Slowly climbing back to her feet, she peered through the snow and trees but couldn't see anything. The horrible chills encompassing her body were nothing to the terror she felt of a bear finding her.

Could the bear smell her? Was he tracking her? She tried to climb the fence one more time, but couldn't even force her hands around the metal. She slid straight to the ground. Slowly bringing her hands to her lips she blew on them to try to restore some movement. Her arms and legs trembled from exhaustion, cold, and terror. She couldn't take it any longer. Unable to force herself to her feet again, she curled into a ball and prayed more diligently. *Let the bear pass me by. Please let him not see me in the storm. Hide me, please, please, please. I'll turn into a stinking saint, I promise.*

She tried to hold her breath, but it was coming so quick and fast she was pretty sure she was going to pass out. Maybe that was okay. If she was going to die at least she'd be blacked out when the bear swiped her head off. Her entire body shook uncontrollably. She cowered against the fence, wanting to bury her head and not see the monster that was coming, but she couldn't do it. Her eyes stayed peeled open, staring into the expanse of white.

A huge brown shape appeared. Maryn bit down so she wouldn't

scream and alert the bear to her presence. As the animal loomed ever closer, Maryn gasped and then started laughing uncontrollably. It was a dog, a huge dog, but still not a bear. A dog she could handle. Even if it wasn't a friendly sort and bit her, it wouldn't shred her to bits.

The dog cocked his head to the side when he noticed Maryn then trotted over to her with tail a wagging and licked her face. Maryn wrapped her arms around his neck and burrowed into his warmth. "Hey there, buddy. You are a sight for sore eyes. Can you help me get to the gate?"

The dog barked as if to say yes. Maryn chuckled and forced herself to stand, luckily her feet held her up even though she couldn't feel them anymore.

This dog was a gift from above. She said a quick prayer of gratitude, but then stiffened. The thumping and breathing was still coming from her left. She swung around to face whatever was coming, clinging to the dog's collar for support. *Please, no.* She'd felt safe for half a minute before that illusion was ripped away. Cold sweat trickled down her chest as she backed away, tugging on the dog who had started barking.

"Quiet, buddy. Let's just find some trees to hide behind or... something." She was a city girl, no clue what to do to protect herself and her new friend.

The bear lumbered into view and all the fear and terror of knowing he was coming didn't compare with the real life horror of staring at an eight-foot grizzly. His paws were immense and nothing in any movie could have prepared her for the claws on the end of those paws. Drool came from his open mouth with teeth that didn't seem to stop. He zeroed in on her and Maryn couldn't even formulate a prayer, all she could hope for was a quick end as her body quivered in fear.

Maryn did the only thing she could possibly do at that moment. She opened her mouth and screamed and screamed and screamed.

The bear seemed to regard her for a moment. The pause stretched her already thin nerves to the breaking point. The dog bared his teeth, growled fearlessly and then leapt at the bear.

"No!" Maryn yelled, reaching out, but only grasping air.

The bear knocked the dog out of the way, batting him like a toy. The dog slammed into the fence and whimpered. His beautiful brown coat shredded and blood dripping down into the white snow.

"Oh, no," Maryn whispered. The poor animal. She ran toward him, but saw the bear raising his paw again. Maryn turned and dove, but she was too slow. The bear's claws lifted her higher off the ground as he swatted her. White-hot pain sliced through her lower back. She could feel every one of those claws as they raked along her skin. Her screaming didn't stop as she hit the ground and splayed there in shock for half a second.

She forced herself to roll over and scamper on hands and knees away from the bear, trying to find somewhere, anywhere to hide. Her back was on fire, the warm blood oozing down her skin in stark contrast to how chilled the rest of her body was.

She glanced back. The bear was moving her direction with his paw raised again. "No!" Maryn shrieked, pushing to her feet and running. She prayed for some hope of safety that may never come. The bear's claws dug into her side and threw her against the fence. She slid down to the ground, a cry of anguish ripping from her body. Curling into a tighter ball, she returned to prayer, but really had no hope of deliverance. Now it was a prayer of, *Please forgive me and take me to be with Thee. Please make this pain stop and get this over quick.* She didn't feel fear of leaving this world, but she didn't want the bear to hit her again. Anything but that.

The Feisty One

A blur of red shot out of the forest along with the loud retort of a gun. Maryn glanced up through bleary eyes. Tucker jumped off a four-wheeler and ran, placing himself between her and the bear.

"No," she whimpered. No matter how grumpy Tucker had been with her, she couldn't stand to see another human be battered like she was.

The bear reared up and let loose a roar that Maryn felt in every inch of her body. Tears streamed down her face, a mixture of the pain she was enduring and dreading Tucker being hurt. The bear would kill him then finish her and there was nothing she could do.

Tucker stood there so courageous and tall, like no man or animal could challenge him. Maryn momentarily forgot her agony as she stared. His hair blew back from his face and his dark eyes were full of determination. Tucker was stronger than Superman to her in that moment and braver than an unarmed warrior against the entire army. Time seemed to freeze as the bear faced off against her personal Beast.

The bear raised his paw and Maryn could hardly stand to watch. Tucker's jaw hardened as he levelled the gun and pulled the trigger. The bear was thrown back toward the trees. The retort of the rifle thundered through the forest and seemed to pulse in Maryn's head.

Tucker fired again. The bear collapsed into a heap of fur and didn't move. Tucker fired one more time then walked over and pushed at the bear with his boot. Seemingly satisfied, he strode back to her. Maryn glanced up and whimpered.

"Oh, Maryn." Tucker set the gun down and lifted her into his arms. His touch on her back sent more pain firing through her body. She buried her head in his chest, not wanting to look at that awful bear. Johnson was calling out to them, but it was coming through a tunnel. Tucker settled onto the four-wheeler and cradled her between his legs as he accelerated away from the carnage.

Maryn glanced up into his handsome face and whispered, "Thank you."

His face was hard as stone until he glanced down at her and his dark eyes softened. "I'm sorry, Maryn."

Maryn tried to smile to reassure him, but the pain was too intense. The cold became unbearable as the four-wheeler picked up speed. Everything grew blurry, but she could still feel warm blood trickling down her side. Darkness filled her mind and she welcomed it with relief.

Chapter Five

Tucker burst through the front door, carrying Maryn in his arms and hoping he wasn't exacerbating her injuries. There was so much blood. Her back and side were both ripped open and he just prayed the claws hadn't penetrated deeply enough to hurt internal organs. The way the snow was pounding outside, he doubted they could make it through the storm to the closest medical center in West Yellowstone before she bled out. Maybe Braxton or Tucker had been able to get through to the emergency dispatcher and help was on its way. He could hope.

"Oh, no!" Mama Porter shrieked when she arrived in the foyer with powdered sugar dusting her apron. Tuck could smell sugar cookies baking and thought how odd it was that something so simple as baking cookies could be happening while a woman's life was on the line. Mama let out another scream then finally managed a coherent, "What on earth happened?"

"Bear," he muttered before turning and barking, "Brax!" He took the stairs two at a time, planning to put her in his bed. Yes, there were seven other bedrooms, but this was his fault and he wanted her close.

Braxton came rushing to his side. His mouth dropped open as he saw Maryn, but he schooled his features quickly. "I'll get the supplies," he murmured and rushed for the basement storage room.

Mama Porter gasped for air as she pumped up the stairs behind Tuck. "Where are you taking her?" she managed to get out.

"My room."

They made it to the third floor without any further conversation as Mama Porter was too out of breath to talk and Tucker was too scared. Maryn hadn't awakened through the cold ride back to the house, all the screaming from Mama Porter, or Tuck carrying her up here.

"Wait!" Mama forced out. "Don't set her down yet."

She ran into his bathroom and returned with a stack of clean sheets. Yanking down the bedspread and comforter she spread out several sheets. "We'll be able to remove them as they get..." Her face paled as she gazed at Maryn. "Soiled."

Tucker nodded and gently laid Maryn on her right side. Her back and left side were raked with long rips from the bears claws. The jacket and shirt were dug into the wounds and blood was everywhere. Luckily there were no gashes on her right or her abdomen. His fingers went to her neck. Her pulse was there, but too slow and faint for his liking. She had to be half-frozen too. He grabbed one of the clean sheets and pressed against her lower back to stop the bleeding.

"Is there time to get her to the hospital?" Mama Porter asked.

The closest hospital was Rexburg, which was a better medical choice than West Yellowstone, but almost a two hour drive in decent weather. "Snow's too thick. We can't risk getting stuck or taking too long to get her help. She might... bleed out. I think it's safer to let Brax doctor her. He's good at stitching." As long as she didn't have any internal injuries. Curse living in such a remote location and curse this snow. There was no way an ambulance or life flight would be getting through.

Mama Porter nodded. "She must be freezing. We've got to get her out of those clothes." She darted a glance at him. "You can't help, it will be unseemly."

The Feisty One

Tucker rolled his eyes. "I think an emergency situation negates social propriety, Mama." He tucked the sheet around her waist, bent down and gently removed Maryn's high-heeled boots, and then peeled off her wet socks. Her feet were white and felt like ice blocks. Tuck rubbed her feet while they waited for Braxton, relieved when some color returned to her toes. Hopefully she wouldn't lose them.

Mama Porter laid a blanket over Maryn then held both of Maryn's small hands between her own, muttering a prayer over and over, "Please help her Lord, please help her." Tucker echoed the prayer in his head. This was all his fault. He'd never forgiven himself for killing innocents years ago in Afghanistan. What would he do if he'd driven this woman from his house and caused injuries that wouldn't heal? What if they lost her? He rubbed her feet harder and muttered a prayer. Not for himself, but for Maryn.

Braxton stormed into the room with Johnson right behind him.

"Any response?" Tuck asked, hoping yet not hopeful.

Johnson shook his head. "I can't get through. Not sure life flight would go out in this anyway."

Tucker nodded, grateful they had Braxton's expertise and were stocked with medical supplies.

"Get me some warm, wet cloths," Brax said to Johnson. "Mama, warm a few blankets in the dryer."

Johnson ran to the bathroom and Mama hurried downstairs. Braxton rolled the blanket off Maryn's upper body and tucked it around her legs then pulled the sheet off and tossed it to the side. Grabbing some scissors, he started cutting Maryn's jacket and shirt. It was awful to watch as a lot of the fabric was dug into her cuts and didn't come out with Braxton's gentle tugs.

Tucker held her body steady on her side. Braxton cut through the front of her clothing and pulled it open then tugged off the material that would come free. "Okay, roll her onto her stomach now, carefully."

They held her like a china doll and placed her on her stomach. Mama returned and placed the warmed blankets over her legs then turned Maryn's head to the side and stroked her cheek. Thankfully, Maryn was still unconscious. Well, maybe that wasn't a good thing. She needed to come around again for him to be grateful for her comatose state at the moment.

Johnson brought warm, wet hand towels and all the men took a different section of Maryn's back, soaking the jacket, blood, and bits of dirt and fur until they could gently pull the fabric out of the gashes. Tuck counted eight spots where the skin had been ripped open. The bleeding had slowed so there was something to be grateful for. Finally, the last piece of material was free and they were able to remove her jacket and shirt.

Johnson helped Braxton set up a suture station. They both snapped on gloves. Braxton irrigated the split flesh while Mama Porter held onto Maryn's cheek with one hand and her cold fingers with the other. Tucker felt so helpless as he continued to rub warmth back into her feet. He made sure the blankets were secure around her wet jeans, thinking they should take them off, but it wouldn't be worth jarring her right now. She looked so pale. He cursed the storm, the bear, and himself. If only they could've gotten ahold of the EMTs. A glance out the window showed nothing but driving white snow and all of their attempts to reach the sheriff earlier had failed. He exhaled and prayed.

"What do you think?" Johnson asked quietly.

Braxton examined each cut and washed them with a wet cloth and more saline. "There's no deep damage and they're clean. I can stitch them as well as anyone could. She's lost a lot of blood and it would be crazy to transport her right now. If she makes it through the night, she'll survive once she gets some antibiotics."

Johnson held the first tear together and Braxton pierced Maryn's flesh with the needle. She jumped and moaned. Tucker hated to think of her in pain, but was glad to see some reaction.

"Hold her!" Braxton commanded. He went back to his supplies and filled a syringe.

"What is that?" Tucker asked.

"Morphine." He gave Tucker a grim smile. "Don't ask where I got it." He shoved it into Maryn's arm and depressed the plunger all the way. She shifted again, but didn't jump. "It's all I've got for pain though, wish I had a local. You and Mama are going to have to hold her tight."

They both nodded. Mama Porter held onto Maryn's delicate shoulders. Tucker laid across her rear and grasped her waist between his hands, determined to hold her steady so Braxton could do what he needed to do. Braxton started stitching again with Johnson holding the wounds closed and also helping to make sure Maryn didn't move. She cried out a few times and tried to squirm away from the needle, but they held her steady. Tucker couldn't stand to watch as the needle worked in and out of her smooth skin. He found that pathetic with all the awful things he'd seen in his life, but this woman had already carved a spot of tenderness out of him.

There were six gashes that needed stitching and it was painfully slow. Finally, Braxton declared it was done. He cleaned off the remaining blood, put Steri-strips on the two smaller cuts, and covered each gash with a large bandage. They left Maryn on her stomach as that seemed the easiest spot for now. Braxton evaluated her fingers and toes. "I don't think she'll have any damage. Mama, can you bring some warm socks and another blanket? We'll cover her up and let her rest."

The morphine must've taken full effect because Maryn didn't respond as they put warm socks on her hands and feet. Braxton covered her up with a sheet and another warm blanket.

"Now we just pray she wakes up in the morning and someone can get through with some antibiotics so she doesn't get infected," Braxton muttered.

Tucker looked sharply at him and Brax shook his head. "Sorry. This is what we're dealing with. You wouldn't want me to sugar coat it."

Tucker nodded, the guilt and anguish eating clear through him.

"One of the biggest side effects of morphine is respiratory depression. We need to monitor her closely," Braxton said.

"We'll take turns watching her through the night." Mama Porter nodded and Tucker could already see her making a chart in her head to make it all fair and even.

"No." Tucker was not leaving her side until she woke up and a doctor snowmobiled in to check her out and give her antibiotics. "I'll stay with her."

Braxton and Mama Porter exchanged glances. Johnson stared at him with that level gaze of a friend who knew what he was dealing with. Only someone who had survived Afghanistan would truly understand.

"Keep trying to get through to the Sheriff or the medical center in West. As soon as a doc or EMT can get in here with some antibiotics and whatever else he thinks she needs, I want him here."

Braxton nodded. He packed up the unused supplies while Mama Porter grabbed a garbage can and Johnson swept the bloodied gauze and ruined clothing into it.

"I brought Max in," Johnson said. "We'll stitch her up and keep her in the lower garage tonight. I think she's going to be okay."

"Max?" Tuck had no idea what his friend was talking about. Why would their dog need stitches?

"The bear got her too. I think she was trying to protect Ms. Howe."

"Oh, Max." The dog loved to explore the Island Park property and was a great companion to all of them. Tucker wished he could bring her upstairs, but he wasn't up for a fight right now. Mama Porter stayed very firm on the no animals in the house rule. "Let me know how she's doing."

Johnson nodded.

They all started to file out, but Mama Porter turned back. "This isn't your fault, Tucker Shaffer and I won't let you blame yourself for it."

Tuck couldn't respond.

Mama Porter patted him on the shoulder. "We'll check on you throughout the night and we'll get a doctor here."

"Thank you." He hung his head, but forced himself to look up and call out to his friend. "Brax."

Braxton pivoted and waited.

"Thank you. I know that wasn't easy." Braxton had been a professional so maybe it was easier than Tucker could imagine, but watching that had made him sick. It was hard to imagine how Braxton kept his hands steady and did such a good job.

Braxton dipped his head in acceptance of the simple gratitude and then followed the others down the stairs.

Tucker glanced over Maryn's still form. She seemed to be sleeping as comfortably as one could whose body had been ripped apart. He pulled an overstuffed leather chair over and sat heavily, knowing this was going to be a miserable night with his demons, regrets, and fears for Maryn and Max's recovery.

The night passed slowly. Mama Porter brought him Dr. Pepper and sugar cookies, muttering about the batch she burned, but he didn't touch any of the food. How could he eat and drink his favorites when Maryn might not survive? He passed a hand over his face. Okay, he was being dramatic and that was a word that had never described him before. Maryn should survive, but she was still in danger of infection or not waking up if she had a concussion and her beautiful body might never be the same again. It made his stomach churn.

Tucker stood and paced next to his bed. Maryn seemed to be resting more easily since the last dose of morphine Braxton administered around three a.m. Thank heavens for Braxton's knowledge and his smuggling of medical supplies from Mexico. Tuck hadn't known about the morphine, but to see Maryn asleep and not writhing in pain was the best sight he could remember.

He studied her face relaxed in sleep. Her features were delicate, from her small nose to her rosebud lips. She was beautiful, but she hadn't acted like the type of woman who used her looks to her advantage. Friendly, open, and fun were probably the words that had best described her before she'd seen those pictures and he'd turned into a growling jerk. How would she react to him when she finally opened her eyes? Tucker dreaded and wished for that moment.

A few times in the night she'd twitch restlessly, her eyelids fluttering, and she would mutter something unintelligible. Tucker hovered, brushing her brow with his fingers and murmuring what he hoped were comforting words, until she settled back down.

The sky lightened outside, signaling the sun had risen, but there was too much snow swirling in the air to see past the river. Tuck heard the high whine of a snowmobile and dropped his head.

"Thank you, Lord." He was surprised at how much he'd prayed tonight. After Afghanistan, he'd given up hope of a higher power ever forgiving him for his sins, but he found he could still beg favors for someone else. He gazed over Maryn. He'd do a lot of things for her he never thought he'd do for anyone and he barely knew her.

A loud rap and then the sound of the doctor and Braxton pounding up the stairs drew his attention. Tucker stood on wobbly legs and met them at the entrance to his suite. He extended his hand. "Thanks for coming."

"Sorry I was so slow. Message just came through a couple hours ago then it was slow going through this storm."

Tucker shot a glance to Braxton who held up his hands. "We've been trying all night. The storm blocked the towers."

Tucker escorted the doctor into his bedroom. Maryn still slept soundly. The doctor checked her pulse and took her temperature before uncovering her back and probing her neck and spine for a few minutes. "I don't feel any misalignment, but when she awakens ask her if she's feeling any pain. If she is, don't move her. We'll have to get an ambulance or helicopter in here somehow and transport her if that's the case."

Tucker's stomach dropped. He hadn't even thought about spinal injury.

The doctor must've noticed his expression. "I think it's unlikely. Just trying to cover all our bases." He carefully peeled back the bandages and checked the sutures. Maryn stirred but didn't awaken. The doctor gave a nod to Braxton. "Experienced hand."

"In another life," Braxton said, but allowed himself a small smile of pride.

"These aren't too deep, they should heal nicely. I wonder if she hit her head when the bear threw her."

"Possibly," Tucker said. "She was up against the fence when I got there."

The doctor nodded. "What have you given her for the pain? Was she lucid enough to take anything?" He smoothed antibiotic cream over the wounds and covered each one back up with fresh gauze.

"No." Braxton studied the winter wonderland outside. "I had some morphine."

"Where did you get morphine?" The doctor arched an eyebrow.

"Mexico."

Both the eyebrows shot up. "Not always the most reliable source for medication. When was her last shot?"

"Three a.m."

"I'll leave another dose for you to administer around ten. Then try to let her wake up and see how she does. I'll leave some oral pain killers. I have Lortab and OxyContin to get you through until you can bring her in tomorrow. If this storm abates. I'll give her a shot of antibiotics and then we'll just watch to make sure no infection manifests. Watch her for nausea, confusion, headaches, the typical concussion signs. Call me if she manifests any of those." He sighed. "The cuts aren't as deep as I feared. She'll be one sore little lady, but if she doesn't have head or spinal injury, she should recover just fine."

Tucker watched silently as the doctor gave Maryn the shot of antibiotics. She didn't respond to the needle at all. Handing all the supplies over to Braxton, the doctor snapped his bag shut and stood.

"What if she doesn't wake up?" Tucker asked.

"There is that, but her vital signs are good and the morphine is keeping her pretty sleepy. Give her until that next dose wears off and if she doesn't start coming around, call me."

Tucker nodded. "Thank you."

The doctor shook his hand then left with Braxton. Tucker sank into the chair again. He recognized his body needed sleep, but he just couldn't allow himself that luxury... not until Maryn opened those blue eyes and reassured him she was okay.

Chapter Six

Everything was hazy. Maryn hated the confusion and cloudiness, but it was so much better than the pain when the bear had ripped her apart and battered her around like a toy. She remembered them stitching her up, though she'd been too worn out and drugged to respond to the ouchiness of the needle pulling in and out of her sensitive skin. After the major pain of the bear attack, the stitches weren't worth complaining about.

There were different voices swirling around her throughout the night, but one was always there, a low almost gravelly voice and the delicious smell that she associated with Tucker. She loved it when she could sense him near, gently touching her, talking to her about who knows what, but it soothed her when she came out of the fog long enough to feel the pain. It felt like the night would never end, but then the room lightened and she sent up a silent prayer of gratitude. She'd survived.

The entire bed smelled like Tucker—a citrus, maybe lime, and she thought it was jasmine and just a hint of salt, like the ocean. She'd never taken the time to dissect how a man smelled, but decided this scent had to be her favorite.

Her feelings were as muddled as her brain, full of pain, fear, and yet that bit of hope. Tucker was her own personal hero. As she dreamed throughout the night, the bear would be chasing her and then Tucker would step in his path, standing as big and burly as the eight-foot bear in her memory. He was her protector.

The feelings of fear she'd associated with him when she saw the photos of those children were now muddled with gratitude and an attraction she couldn't deny. James was always so polished in his suits with his fake-tanned skin and blond hair slicked back. He was definitely a dapper kind of handsome and she had thought she was attracted to him, but the raw masculinity that was Tucker Shaffer couldn't be competed with.

Maryn wanted to climb out of this fog and find out more about the man. There had to be an explanation for what was written on the back of those photos and his reaction to her seeing them. She just knew it and maybe tomorrow she'd be awake enough and brave enough to chat with Tucker and he'd reveal everything she was dying to know. But for now whatever they'd injected into her arm was taking effect and sleep sounded wonderful.

After Braxton had given Maryn more morphine and Mama Porter had refreshed Tucker's untouched drink around ten, he'd heard Brax and Mama Porter talking just outside the room.

"I've never seen him like this," Mama Porter said.

"Do you think he cares for her?" Braxton asked. "I thought he might be past caring for anyone but the three of us."

"A body can only hope something will crack his heart," Mama Porter said.

Tuck ran a hand through his hair. It didn't matter what he thought about the beautiful creature suffering in his bed. Maryn thought he was a monster and he doubted anything would change her mind.

Tucker looked down at her petite features and that cloud of

blonde hair. She moaned and rolled to her side. Tucker wanted to stop her, but she rolled to her right side and that shouldn't hurt her. The sheet slipped down to reveal the smooth skin of her shoulder. Tucker lifted the sheet and blanket back up to cover her, resisting the urge to touch that creamy skin. He didn't want to stare at her in only her bra and intrude on her privacy. She seemed very... pure.

Maryn blinked and her blue eyes were dull but still very intriguing. "Tucker?" she croaked. She licked her lips. "I'm not dead?"

He grunted out a surprised laugh. "No, thank heavens."

"The dog?"

"She's doing okay too. They stitched her up and she's running around in the garage tearing things apart and driving Braxton crazy. Her name is Max." Tucker usually didn't ramble on, but his relief at seeing her awake had him more excited than he'd been in a long time.

"Max." She smiled, but it obviously took a lot of effort. "I'm glad he's okay. Can I steal some water?"

Tucker laughed. "You can have all you want for free." Grabbing a water bottle off the dresser he held it to her lips, squirting a little bit in at a time until she nodded slightly.

She gave him a faint smile, obviously still cloudy from the drugs. "I prayed pretty hard, and He sent me you..." Her voice trailed off, but he clearly heard her whisper, "You are my hero."

Tuck swallowed hard, grateful she'd fallen asleep again and he didn't have to reply to that comment. He used to think he was a hero and look where it had gotten him. He wasn't sure he wanted to be a hero anymore.

Maryn opened her eyes to see Tucker studying her from the chair next to her bed.

"You're awake again?" he said, his voice pitching up in a happy tone.

This huge man with the piercing dark eyes kept surprising her. She needed to get to the bottom of his secrets and see what kind of man he really was. A stinking handsome and tough dude that was for sure.

"Can I get you anything?" he asked.

Maryn shook her head, but then nodded as she remembered James. He would probably come up here and storm the house if she didn't report in. They usually talked several times a day and the last thing she'd said to him yesterday was that the guard dog was coming and then she'd hung up on him and silenced her phone. Not very nice. "I need to get a hold of my... publisher. He'll be stressing out."

"We haven't been able to make calls until this morning. Do you know where your phone is?"

Maryn closed her eyes, remembering. "It was in the pocket of my jacket. Did you throw away all my clothes?" How embarrassing that she was next to naked under these blankets. Who had been checking her out? At least she had on a favorite red and white swirled bra with decent coverage of essentials.

"They cut them off you, but I don't think there was a phone. It must've fallen out in the snow. Do you know your publisher's number?"

"No. It's programmed in my phone."

"Johnson can find it. He works with the PR people who set up the interview. We'll get a message to your editor."

"Thanks." Her eyelids were starting to droop. "That would be perfect if you'd just call *The Rising Star* and let them know what happened. Tell them to let James know I'm okay."

"Sure."

"Oh, and Tucker," she forced herself to stay awake. "I need to know something."

"Yes." He glanced down at her, so concerned and protective. She licked her lips and said, "What brand of cologne do you wear? It's killing me."

Tucker chuckled. He brushed some hair from her face and she trembled in response. "Giorgio Armani. Mama Porter gave me a bottle for Christmas one year and I liked it, so I kept buying it."

"It blends perfectly with your chemistry. I mean, you smell perfect and I want to keep smelling it. I mean." Maryn closed her eyes and sank into the pillows. "I am drugged and exhausted, forget everything I said."

Tucker laughed and pulled the covers up, brushing his hand along her shoulder. Maryn knew she had some kind of diagnosable complex where you fall for your rescuer, but if he smelled and looked this good and was filthy rich to boot, who could blame her? The girls from Camp Wallakee would be proud she was interested in a billionaire and Alyssa would be shocked. She fell asleep with a smile on her face.

Chapter Seven

Braxton reported to the doctor that Maryn had awakened and didn't show any signs of a concussion or spinal injury. Tucker smiled. Unless rambling on about how he smelled perfect counted as confusion. The doctor instructed that if she felt good enough and the plows had been able to clear the roads of the snow that had piled up and was still continuing to fall, they should bring her into the medical center in West Yellowstone tomorrow. Braxton came and checked her stitches, applying more antibacterial cream, and then covering them back up with clean gauze.

Maryn stirred and muttered, "How crappy do they look?"

"You're actually looking really good, ma'am. I'm grateful they weren't deeper. Is your pain manageable?"

"Sure, if you're a sado-masochist."

Braxton gave a grunt that almost sounded like a laugh. Maryn didn't respond again, so she must've fallen back to sleep. "She's an interesting one, isn't she?" Braxton said.

"Sure, if you're into gorgeous, funny, blonde reporters," Tuck said then instantly regretted his words as Braxton arched an eyebrow. He could've sworn that Maryn smiled.

Braxton packed up his supplies, nodded to Tucker then left the room. Tucker settled in to wait for Maryn to awaken again. It was slow going. The morphine must've worn off in the early afternoon because she started moaning a bit more and then she opened her eyes, focused on Tucker and whispered, "It hurts."

Tucker was tempted to give her more of Braxton's contraband morphine. "The doctor wanted us to ease you off the morphine and try something else. Are you allergic to any pain meds?"

"No."

"Okay, let's try the stronger of the two then." He took the cup with the OxyContin in it, grateful it was also a smaller pill. Now the trouble was to get her vertical enough to swallow a pill.

She pushed with her arm to try to lift herself up and cried out.

"Wait," Tucker begged. He hurried to the bed and held on to her uninjured right side and lifted her up just enough before handing her first the pill and then the water bottle.

She swallowed it quickly and he settled her back onto her side. "Thank you."

The blanket had slipped down, revealing a very nice shape and a red and white swirled bra. How had Tucker not noticed that last night? He looked away. "Can I... adjust anything to make you more comfortable?"

"Um." She glanced down and then lifted the sheet back over her abdomen. "I need to use the bathroom and it would be heaven to get out of these pants. They feel like they're sewn to my butt."

He couldn't help but laugh. She phrased things in a way that was so uniquely Maryn. "Okay. I'll get Mama Porter and we'll get you to the bathroom then she can help you... take care of stuff. Johnson brought your bag from your car."

"That's crack-a-lackin. Thank you."

He ran to the panel on the wall, and depressed the button for the kitchen. "Mama, she's awake and needs help using the bathroom." He couldn't keep the excitement out of his voice. Maryn was fully awake and using her funny expressions. She was going to be okay. Maybe he'd get a chance to talk to her soon. If he begged her forgiveness would it ever come? His heart sank. He couldn't forgive himself for Afghanistan so what made him think she could forgive him? And she was a reporter. Of course she'd want to know all about the photographs or make up her own story based on incomplete data.

Mama Porter huffed into the room, obviously having run up the stairs. All this drama was giving her more exercise than she'd had in years. "Oh, darling girl, you're awake."

Maryn smiled at her. "I think sleep hurt less. Wanna knock me out again?"

Tucker grinned, but sobered quickly, he hated her being in pain.

"Oh, I'll bet you're hurting, but you're going to heal up just fine. Now let's get you up and into the bathroom. I can't believe you've waited this long to go."

"I've got the bladder of a camel," Maryn said.

Tucker laughed.

Mama Porter shook her head, smiling. "Well, I guess that's a good thing. Now Tuck, lift her up, gently, gently."

Tucker placed his hands under Maryn's armpits and along her upper back, careful to avoid looking at or touching anything he shouldn't, and easily lifted her onto her feet. She grimaced but said, "Thank you. That hurt a lot less than me trying to strain."

He held onto her arm on one side and Mama Porter braced her on the other. They made it into his master bath and the women went into the private toilet. Tucker hurried back to the bedroom and grabbed her bag. He opened it to find her something more comfortable to wear, but blushed when he pulled out a pair of bright blue, silky underwear. This woman certainly liked color. Closing the bag, he set it on the counter and hurried out of the bathroom. He shut the door and waited on the other side. He'd go in if they needed him, but he didn't want to make Maryn, or himself, uncomfortable. Her bra wasn't any more revealing than many swimsuits he'd seen, but he hadn't been around a beautiful woman in a while. That had to account for his awkwardness.

Maryn let out some obvious squeaks of pain, but Mama Porter's soothing voice came through and he found himself grateful Maryn was so small and Mama was so solid. He listened as water ran and counted the seconds until he could help somehow.

"Tuck," Mama called out.

Tucker opened the door and found Maryn dressed in a pair of pink and green plaid pajama bottoms and a loose-fitted green tank top. Her face was washed clean of the makeup smudges and Mama was securing her long hair in a ponytail. She looked fresh and gorgeous.

"I think we've worn her out," Mama Porter said. "Can you lift her without touching her stitches?"

"I'm not a complete wuss. I can crawl back to the bed," Maryn said, tilting her chin up.

Tucker crossed the bathroom in three long strides and looked down at her. "I never tell Mama no," he said, liking how small she was next to him. The desire to protect a woman, other than Mama Porter, had never been this strong.

Maryn arched her delicate eyebrows. "I wouldn't want to strain any of those muscles."

Tucker chuckled out loud. "Because you probably weigh all of a hundred pounds."

"A hundred and fifteen thank you very much. I work hard for this body." She lifted her left arm like she was going to flex it, but cried out, her smooth face contorted in pain. The movement must've tugged at the stitches. "Remind me to use my right side next time."

Tucker felt her pain like it was his own. How could he have done this to her? He came around to her right side and placed one arm under her shoulders, thankful the gashes were down low. Tucking the other arm underneath her thighs, he easily swung her off the ground and close to his body. She rested her head against his chest. He knew it was probably because she was exhausted, but the sweetness of her movement had all kinds of protective urges firing through him.

The walk back to the bed was much too short. He gently laid her on her right side and then bent down close. Her eyes were fastened on his face. They'd been so blue earlier but now in the green tank top they looked almost an aqua green.

"I'm so sorry," he whispered.

She shook her head. "It wasn't your fault."

"If I wouldn't have scared you... or if I'd gotten there sooner."

She touched his cheek with her soft fingers. The warmth of her hand shot through him. He covered her hand with his own.

"You're a hero, Tucker Shaffer, and don't you dare think any differently."

Tucker turned her hand over and kissed her palm then set it down. Her cheeks flushed and he was certain he'd never seen anything more beautiful.

"Now," Mama Porter said behind them. "Does any food sound good to you, my dear?"

Tucker's stomach grumbled and Maryn laughed, a delightful sound that lightened Tucker's very existence. "I think Tucker should scarf down a pig or maybe a cow, but I'm happy to just have some more water."

"What about some broth and juice?"

"I could try that."

"I'll bring up food for both of you." Mama hurried out of the room and they were left staring at each other.

"So what do we do now?"

"Um, let you rest and heal?"

"No. I'm talking about all the questions I have that you are going to answer."

Tuck's chest tightened. She was beautiful and innocent and... still a reporter. "Barely awake from a traumatic accident and already wanting to get my dirt?"

Maryn studied him with those bluish-green eyes. "I want to know about you. Not for an article. I would never exploit you because you're my personal hero and because... I've never been more intrigued by a man."

Tucker leaned toward her, barely resisting touching the smooth skin of her cheek. "I'm no hero, Maryn. I'm..." He cleared his throat. "I'm sorry I reacted the way I did and scared you."

"Thank you. I can trust that you won't do it again and you can trust me enough to talk to me."

He leaned back in his chair, not sure what to think. He liked that she'd moved on so quickly from his terrifying behavior yesterday, but could he share personal things with this woman? Would she sell his secrets for her own success or was she truly intrigued by him? Maryn seemed very genuine, but it could be an act to get him to spill.

"Trust is hard for me," he whispered.

"I can see that. You've surrounded yourself with the three people you trust and you shut everyone else out. Why Tucker? Why shut out the world?"

The Feisty One

He shrugged and clasped his hands together, studying a scar on his right thumb. One of the few scars that wasn't from Afghanistan but from childhood—one of his foster brothers had dared him to climb a barbed wire fence and it hadn't turned out well. "The world's a scary place, Maryn Howe."

She laughed, that tinkling sound that he wanted to hear the rest of his life. "I can't imagine a tough Army veteran being afraid of anything. You just stood in front of a grizzly bear and protected me." She shivered as she said the words grizzly bear.

Tuck's head jerked up. "How'd you know I was an Army veteran?"

"I'm good at research." She paused then whispered, "I'll sign a statement that I will only paint you in a good light, will not reveal anything you don't want me to reveal, and will share the article with you before publication so you can approve it. If I fail on any of those things you can sue me. I have an adorable green Volkswagen bug and a closet full of clothes and shoes that many women would give up their eyelashes for."

Tucker laughed. "You want me to trust you and spill all of my secrets then you'll make me look like a hero for your article?" Truly though, what could she print that would be any worse than what had already happened? She knew about the pictures. It was probably less risky to answer her questions and hope she could somehow forgive him and maybe even learn to like him a little bit.

She licked her lips and focused on him. "It's not about the article, Tucker. I won't even write if it you don't want me to. I don't care if James fires me. It's about you... and me."

Tucker looked at her, wondering how much of what she was saying was induced by medication or gratitude that he'd saved her from the bear. "You're a blunt one, aren't you?"

67

"I have been accused of that a time or two."

"Can you call me Tuck?"

"Tuck," she breathed out his name and Tucker realized if she hadn't been injured he would've pulled her into his arms and tasted those rosebud lips. His stomach did a weird lurch and his palms started sweating as she stared into his eyes and didn't look away.

Mama Porter brought their food and found the two of them in a staring contest that he didn't want to end.

Mama babied Maryn through the short meal and to her credit, Maryn didn't complain, though she did roll her eyes or pull a face at Tuck a couple of times. "That's enough, thank you," Maryn said, obviously exhausted after sitting up to drink some broth and eating a few pieces of cheese and orange.

Mama helped her lay back down and then took her tray to the kitchen. "I'll be back for yours in a minute," she told Tucker.

"I can bring it down. Thank you, Mama."

She nodded, smiling as she looked back and forth between the two of them for a minute then disappeared out the door.

Maryn closed her eyes and lay still. Tuck felt instant relief that the questions were put on hold for a little while. He wanted to trust her, to share with her, but it was terrifying at the same time. There were parts of his story that not even Mama Porter and Braxton knew. Johnson was the only one who could relate and commiserate.

"Don't think you're off the hook, big guy," Maryn whispered sleepily. "I'm taking a short nap then I'm done with this wallowing in pain, and my focus is on getting to know my new friend, Tuck."

Tuck couldn't resist leaning forward, brushing the hair from her face, and kissing her cheek. Maryn's lips turned up in a smile.

"I think we're going to be good friends, you and I," Maryn said then her breathing evened out and within thirty seconds she was snoring.

Tuck chuckled to himself. This tiny beauty snored? Who would've guessed that? He liked that he knew that about her but liked even more that she did it. He ate all of his chicken noodle soup and ham sandwich then allowed himself to lean back in the chair and watch her sleep. His eyelids drifted closed and he'd never felt so at peace in his life.

Chapter Eight

Maryn's eyes flittered open and she forgot for a second why she was in this huge, comfortable bed that smelled like a fine-looking member of the male species, looking out windows with nothing but white. Then she saw Tucker, fast asleep in an overstuffed chair and smiled. The memory of why she got in this bed wasn't good, but she was excited to get to know this man better. She'd been much too forward earlier when she'd told him her desire to learn everything, but he'd have to believe she was drug-addled and forgive her. Not that she'd give up on her quest to know this man's secrets. Amazingly, it wasn't for the article, but because Tuck was so impressive.

She moved to rub her hands together like she always did when she was excited and bit her lip to hold in the cry of pain. Okay, don't stretch the arms too far. She was feeling pretty good for someone who was attacked by a bear only the night before. Her head was a little woozy still and her body ached like she'd been beat up, but as long as she didn't move in certain ways the stitches weren't bad.

Mama Porter and Tuck had treated her like an invalid after she used the bathroom. She grinned. Not that she'd minded Tuck picking her up in those burly arms and then kissing her on the cheek. The attraction between them was like nothing she'd experienced before. Laying her head on his chest had been a natural action and wowzers, what a chest it was. James was the only man she'd been close to the past few months and though he had a nice build it was a honed in the gym and on a surfboard kind of build. Tuck's strength was part of who he was. She wouldn't be surprised if he chopped wood every morning and slung bales of hay around.

Ha! Like billionaire Tucker Shaffer was a part-time farmer.

She pushed her way to sitting and only cried out a little. Tuck jumped from his chair, landing in a half-crouch with his hands splayed out. "Don't move. I'll help you."

Maryn laughed. "I'm fine, Tuck."

His dark eyes swung over her frame and for some reason Maryn blushed. Straightening and lowering his hands, he said, "You're fine, but you're not fine."

"Now that made sense," she teased.

He grinned. "What do you need?"

"I'm just ready to stand up and move around a bit. My hip fell asleep from lying on my side."

"Okay. Should I lift you or just support you?"

Maryn thought of those large hands lifting her out of the bed earlier. She didn't want to be a wussy female, but he *was* very capable. "Just do what you did earlier. That didn't hurt the stitches."

Wrapping his hands underneath her arms, he easily lifted her to solid footing. Her face was inches away from his chest. Maryn glanced up, holding his gaze and enjoying having him near when she was upright and semi-lucid.

"Thanks," she whispered, her voice much huskier than it should've been. She cleared her throat.

Tuck stepped back and grabbed a water bottle. "Do you need this?"

She nodded. Tuck lifted it to her lips and squeezed a bit in.

Earlier he'd done something similar to give her pain meds, but it hadn't felt nearly so intimate.

"Do you want to just stand for a few minutes?" He grasped her right elbow as if to support her.

Maryn should've told him she didn't need him to hold her up, she was feeling okay just standing here, but she liked his touch too much to say anything. "Could we go down to the basement and check on Max? I want to thank him for saving my life."

"I thought I was the one who saved your life." The glint in Tucker's eyes told her he was teasing. "Are you sure you're up to that many stairs?"

"If I'm not, I'm sure you'll carry me."

He lifted his eyebrows and then swept her off her feet before she could tell him she'd been teasing. Maryn couldn't lift her hands too high without tugging at unhealed flesh so she placed them both against that well-formed chest. Tuck grinned down at her and walked toward the stairs.

"Okay. That worked out well for me. I might have to keep you around as my own personal body lifter."

Tuck chuckled. "You don't strike me as the helpless sort."

"True. But you have to admit this is kinda fun." She licked her lips and blinked up at him.

"More than kinda," he whispered, almost too quiet for her to hear.

Maryn leaned in close to him so she didn't keep flirting and embarrass him too much as he easily descended the four sets of stairs to reach the basement. This house was a bit massive for her, but she wasn't going to complain about all this time spent in Tuck's arms. Her heart was beating quickly and happy nerve endings instead of the stinking pain receptors were firing at triple speed.

72

At the far north side of the sprawling basement there was an entrance to a lower garage. The space was full of snowmobiles, four-wheelers, side by sides, and a brown dog.

The dog ran up to them. Tuck sat Maryn on her feet and she bent down and gently stroked his head. "Max. Thank you."

Max tilted his head up and barked. Tucker buried his fingers in the dog's fur. "She's a good pup, isn't she?"

"She? You've been letting me call a girl a boy and what kind of a name is Max for a girl?"

"Maxine," Tuck explained. "After Johnson's favorite grandmother. I think I told you earlier, but you were pretty drugged."

"Gotcha." Maryn shook her head. She glanced over the dog's body, seeing bits of shaved fur and stitches. "Did she suffer much?"

"She did fine. Braxton took good care of her and you can see she's already running around like nothing happened."

"What a good girl." Maryn stroked her head some more, but then her legs wobbled and she would've fallen if Tuck hadn't wrapped an arm around her shoulders and held on. "Whew and I haven't even been drinking."

Tuck held her steady for a second. "You're trying to do too much, let's get you back to bed."

"No, please. Couldn't we go sit in your lovely sunroom for a bit?"

Tuck gently lifted her off her feet and carried her back up the stairs. Maryn was feeling tired, but she was not ready to lie back in the bed. She wanted to talk to Tuck and pretend everything was normal for a minute. He walked through the main area and Mama Porter beamed at them from the kitchen. "Oh, it's good to see you up and about."

"I'm not really up. Tuck's having to carry me everywhere like a baby."

"You'll get your strength back soon." She bustled from one pot to the other. "Supper's almost ready. Do you want me to bring it upstairs?"

"Sure," Tuck said.

"Could we please eat in the sunroom again?" Maryn asked him.

"Um, sure. If you're feeling up to it."

Mama Porter opened the door for them and Tuck settled her into a comfortable chair. She had to be careful not to put too much pressure on her back or left side, but it felt good to be sitting up. She glanced out the windows at a vastly different scene from yesterday when they'd had dinner in here. The sun was still obscured by clouds and everything was covered in soft white. The trees all had a comfortable blanket of snow and the river trickled merrily with ice on the edges and snow covering any exposed rocks.

"It's beautiful," Maryn said, "but who gets snow in October?"

"Crazy, huh? But I like it. It's very different from our other homes."

"You say ours like this isn't all yours."

"It's not." He studied her and took a long breath before admitting, "Brax, Johnson, and Mama all own shares of my properties and a lot of my investments and products are in their names."

Maryn leaned back in surprise. Pain shot through her lower back and she quickly righted herself, swallowing a murmured ouch. "Why?" He'd said something yesterday about putting different products in their names, but she hadn't realized to what extent he'd shared his wealth.

"I'd have none of this without them, especially Johnson who's the reason Friend Zone is so successful." He shook his head. "Johnson would be the first to say he didn't do much, but he did and without Johnson and Brax's business sense and all of them believing in me I would've given up a long time ago."

Maryn shook her head. "You've got a backbone of steel Tucker Shaffer. I don't think the word give up is in your vocabulary."

He rubbed his hand along the metal table and didn't respond.

"Why is Johnson the reason for Friend Zone's success?"

He leaned back in his chair. "Are you up for a story?"

Maryn nodded. "You know I love stories."

"I don't know near enough about you, Maryn." His dark eyes bore into her as if challenging her to spill all her secrets. She was definitely tempted.

"If you're a good boy, I might tell you more."

Tuck arched an eyebrow and smiled. The little scar appeared at the corner of his lip and Maryn had a hard time not licking her lips.

"I look forward to it." He paused and said, "Tell me just one secret about you, something not many people know about Maryn Howe."

Maryn smiled, liking that he wanted to know. She thought for a minute. He didn't need to hear her boo-hoo of a childhood, wishing she had a dad, being poor, watching her mom clean and sometimes be a step above a prostitute to improve their situation, Alyssa and her father giving Maryn what her mom couldn't and then Alyssa's dad turning into a scumbag. She wondered about that one, maybe he was a scumbag all along and they just hadn't recognized it until they grew older. Thinking of Alyssa and her dad, reminded her of a story she could share.

"My best friend's dad used to pay for me to go to girl's camp with her every summer. I met some of my best friends during those weeks." She thought about all of them. Besides Facebook posts and messages, she really only stayed in touch with Alyssa, Haley, and MacKenzie. Haley came to visit occasionally. She would take her adorable boy to Disneyland and stay at Maryn's apartment to save money. "One night, Erin, she was kind of our official leader, came up with a silly pact. We all swore we were going to marry billionaires or we'd have to sing the Camp Wallakee song at our wedding."

Tucker tilted his head to the side. "There aren't that many billionaires in the world."

"Not that I've met."

"Lucky you met me." He blushed and rushed on, "Singing a camp song doesn't seem like an awful punishment for failing."

Maryn thought it was very lucky she met him, but not because of the Billionaire Bride Pact. She couldn't care less if she ever fulfilled it. "We were twelve and on a sugar rush. But you should hear the song, it's wicked embarrassing, there are even these screeching caws at the end, and we can't tell anyone why we're singing it."

"That would be embarrassing."

"Yeah, it would." She shifted in her chair and tried not to wince. "But I always argued that my idea was a better punishment," she rushed on so Tuck wouldn't say something about her hurting. "I said if we didn't marry a billionaire the punk we married had better be a hottie and all the other girls got to kiss our husband at our wedding."

"Seems like a punishment for the husband."

"No, my friends are cute." She winked.

Tuck elevated his eyebrows. "So if you marry a billionaire it's only for the money because he couldn't possibly be a hottie?"

Maryn blushed. "No, no. I was just young and saying if the

dude was poor he'd better be cute, but after meeting you I realize you can be a billionaire and a hottie too. I mean." Her eyes widened. "Well, I didn't mean, but I did mean. Oh, heavens." Her tongue was looser than ever. She needed to stop all pain meds.

Tuck grinned. "So, do you plan on marrying a billionaire?"

"No." She shook her head, though she couldn't resist watching his reaction. He leaned closer to her and waited. "It's more of a joke to me. Some of my friends have married wealth. One's already divorced, but my best friend Alyssa is really happy. No, the pact is more something for my boyfriend to tease me about..." She trailed off again as his eyes widened.

"You have a boyfriend?"

"No, um, not really." Okay, no more pain meds no matter how bad it hurt. How could she have said something about James? "I'm going to stop talking now."

"How do you 'not really' have a boyfriend?" His dark eyes were so intense and probing hers as if he could read the deeper meaning she didn't want to explain.

Maryn decided honesty was the only option she had if she wanted Tucker to share things with her. "My editor, James." She sighed then continued, "We date off and on and he asks me to marry him all the time, but it's not like a boyfriend because I've never allowed it to be, even though he wants it to be. He's just a really good friend who has always been there for me. You probably think I'm awful, flirting with you when I may or may not have a boyfriend."

"I don't think you're awful, I just... hoped you were unattached."

"I am." She smiled, hoping he would believe her. She had vowed in her terror of the bear attack to marry James, but she

77

thought the Lord would understand she wasn't ready for marriage. She could be a saint on her own. "It's more of a convenience thing for both of us. We work together so it's easy to go to parties or dinner and sometimes he tries to make more of it than there is. I've only kissed him a few times and it wasn't that fabulous." Her cheeks reddened but she was committed now. "We don't have the... sparks that a couple who's dating should have." The sparks she'd felt with the man seated across from her who she barely knew and he hadn't even tried to kiss her. Except on the hand and the cheek. She savored those remembrances.

He nodded, but seemed unconvinced.

"So, you got your Maryn Howe secret, please tell me a story." Maryn was dying to know more about him. "You and Johnson?"

He clasped his hands together. "It's kind of a long story."

"Perfect." Better if she didn't talk and say anything else that might push this man away. She wanted to grow closer to him in every sense of the word. Shifting in her seat to get more comfortable, she ignored the wave of exhaustion.

"Are you feeling okay?"

"I'm awesome." She was a liar and his eyes said he knew that. "Story, please."

"Okay." He studied her for a few seconds, shook his head, and then began, "My dream my entire life was to play football. San Diego Chargers were my team."

"Really? They haven't been that great."

"I know, but you've got to be loyal to your team."

"True. Broncos fan myself."

"Not a bad choice. If you would've said Raiders I might've thrown you out of the house." His cheek crinkled when he grinned.

"Ha! No worries. They're at the bottom of the pile for me." She paused then said, "So when did you start playing football?"

The Feisty One

"Never. None of my foster parents would pay the fees and I was too shy to ask for assistance at school." He glanced down again. "I was a really chubby kid and got teased a lot so I withdrew into computer games."

Maryn swallowed. Her heart went out to a young Tucker, shuffled from home to home, overweight and awkward and nobody cared enough to pay for his dreams. So sad.

"I started having all kinds of ideas for how I could improve the games I was playing, so I began designing code and getting involved in a lot of online sites that taught me what to do. I created a few games that made a little money, enough that I bought my own Mac and could hole up in my room and work for hours on end." He stood and started pacing the room.

Maryn loved his energy. She couldn't imagine how this strong body could be holed up, miserable and overweight and designing computer games for hours on end. "Did they even check on you?"

He shrugged. "None of my families were awful to me. They were just busy and figured they'd done me a favor giving me shelter, food, and clothing. Usually they appreciated how quiet and easy I was. I'd only get moved to a new home when there were overcrowding issues."

Maryn repositioned herself in her seat. It was hard to not be able to relax fully against the cushions.

"Are you sure you're doing okay?" Tuck was next to her chair in a second.

"I'm good," she reassured him. "The story is taking my focus off of my back. Is that why you don't like attention now?"

He nodded and settled back into his seat, looking pleased that she seemed to understand. "When you're a kid that basically hides in the background, it's weird to have all these people suddenly care what you're wearing, who you're talking to, what you're saying. Just because I came up with an idea and I have lots money."

"Our society is messed."

Looking at his clasped hands, he exhaled slowly then muttered, "Inside, I still feel like that little boy sometimes."

Mayrn loved that he told her that. "Well, you've grown into yourself nicely."

Tucker chuckled, met her gaze, and licked his lips. "Thank you."

She cleared her throat, embarrassed that she couldn't help but compliment him, but he was miles from that chubby kid who hid with his computer. "So after you graduated high school?"

"I got a scholarship to go to college, but I found out I could have even more benefits if I joined the Army. I really liked the idea of being active, of someone whipping me into shape. I went to the University of Idaho, up in Moscow, and that's when I met Johnson. We were trained as snipers together and ended up being roommates. He was social and fun and everyone just loved him. I always claimed it was the dimples."

"It's hard to not like those dimples."

Tuck arched an eyebrow at her. She rushed to say, "Not that I would want a man with dimples they just... make him more approachable."

Tucker's eyes laughed at her, but luckily he was too much of a gentleman to question her about what she would want in a man. "They do. I designed Friend Zone hanging out at our apartment and listening in while all of Johnson's friends used social media and praised or complained about different aspects of every site."

"Some people say you were the ultimate copycat."

"Oh, for sure. I took bits and pieces from every site and some ideas of my own and made it work. Johnson and his friends tested it for me for a year then I got deployed. Johnson made it to Afghanistan about six weeks after me. About a year later, we were in the middle of staking out a cave in the middle of the desert where many Al Qaeda leaders were supposed to be hiding. He turns to me and says, 'Hey, I forgot to tell you, that site you designed, we did a huge shout out for it and I think you're pretty wealthy now.'"

Tucker shook his head. "Biggest shock of my life when I found out his shout out got me a million subscribers within a few days and then the thing went viral and it's had huge success ever since. I can't believe Johnson waited that long to tell me, but he said he was waiting for a moment when I really needed it."

He passed a hand over his chin. "Johnson gave Shane, one of his buddies, access to everything on the back end. He was our customer service and troubleshooter for the eighteen months we were deployed. Shane fixed so many problems. Dropped out of school because he was working so hard. We paid him ten million dollars and he's never complained. Shane got a degree in Phys. Ed, married, and has three boys. He coaches a bunch of little league baseball teams to give his wife a little bit of space. It's weird to be semi-retired at twenty-five."

Maryn's eyes widened. "Wow. I am eating this up! So, you're out sweating in the sand watching this cave for terrorists and Johnson drops that on you. What happened then?"

His mouth turned down. "We were hiding in a cave ourselves. We waited for days. It was miserable and hot and we were going out of our heads." He paused and studied his hands. "Our orders were to shoot every person that came out of the opening."

Her heart constricted in her chest. The pictures she'd seen. "Did you?" she whispered through a very dry throat.

Tuck dropped his head. "Yes." After several long seconds, he glanced back up at her. "I'm a monster, Maryn. I didn't want you to know."

Maryn shook her head. "I can't imagine how hard it was for you."

"It was dark when they came out. Looking through the night vision goggles distorts things and they were all armed. It's no excuse." He studied her for a second as if gauging her reaction. "I was so ready to finally be fulfilling the assignment, I didn't pay attention to who or what I was shooting." He ran his hands through his long hair. "It's what we were trained for."

"What happened when you realized it?" She felt so guilty asking more of him, but it seemed like he needed to get it out.

"Johnson and I both saw therapists. They discharged us early because of mental instability. It was tough."

"How did you get the pictures?"

He cleared his throat. "Computer geek, remember?" He gave a self-deprecating shake of his head. "I knew the Army was scoping out that cave. I cracked into the satellite imaging and went back over the two weeks before our hit. We did end up taking out a bunch of Al Qaeda leaders, but I found and printed off the pictures of the children. There were seven..." He trailed off.

Maryn swallowed and whispered, "You did that to yourself?"

He nodded, pressing his lips together.

"Oh, Tucker, I wish I could help."

He met her gaze. His eyes so full of sadness, regret, and self-recrimination. "Are you offering?"

Maryn smiled to try to lighten the mood. "I'm no professional, but I do know how to pray pretty good."

Tucker arched an eyebrow. "The Lord doesn't want to hear from me."

"You're wrong. He wants you more than you understand."

Mama Porter bustled through the door supporting a tray overflowing with yummy smells. Tucker seemed to breathe a sigh of relief. He jumped up to help Mama and then served Maryn the tantalizing boneless spare ribs, red potatoes, broccoli, and homemade rolls.

"Thank you," Maryn called to Mama as she hurried away again. "I hope she doesn't spoil you like this all the time."

Tucker shook his head. "Only when we have a guest." He cracked a smile. "And we never have guests."

"Well, I feel privileged." Yet she didn't feel like a guest. She felt like part of a family, something she'd only dreamt of. She tried to cut some meat. Tucker stood and cut everything up for her. "I feel like a little child," she complained.

"You don't like anyone taking care of you, do you?"

Maryn bit at her lip. "Never really had anyone taking care of me, well, besides Alyssa."

"You mentioned her before. Tell me about Alyssa." Tucker sat down and tore a bite off the roll.

"We've been best friends our whole lives. Kept each other alive through college and starting careers. She's a sweetie and an amazing photographer. You have one of her pictures in your room. The one of the old man and little girl."

"She's A.A.?"

"Yes."

"That's crazy. I have some more of her work in my Laguna Beach house. I like the way she captures people."

Maryn nodded. The bite of ribs melted in her mouth. "She's super talented, but she got married this past summer so I'm a loner again."

"The men in L. A. must be idiots if you're a loner."

Maryn smiled. She wasn't a loner because she couldn't get dates, but because she really didn't have the deep, lasting relationships she dreamed of. James and Alyssa had always been there for her, but the rest of her friends were more fun or convenience. James was probably worried sick. She hadn't called him yesterday. "Did you get a hold of James?"

Tucker's eyes darkened. "James, the boyfriend?"

"No, James my publisher." And semi-boyfriend, but she didn't want to get into that again.

"Yeah, Johnson said he got a message through and they were concerned for you and wanted him to keep them up to date. I'll make sure he calls again tonight."

"Thank you." James' blue eyes and blonde hair were getting a bit fuzzy as she stared at the dark-haired man before her. Alyssa's Granny Ellie would say Tucker was, "Lots of man." She smiled to herself. She missed Granny Ellie, who had passed away last spring. Alyssa and her husband, Beckham, were in Honduras for a few more weeks so they wouldn't notice if Maryn didn't respond to an email or text for a couple of days. How was she going to find all her contacts with her cell phone missing?

"What's the frown for?" Tucker asked, taking a drink of water.

"Just thinking about what a pain it's going to be losing my cell phone. Without the SIM card I won't have any of my contacts."

"If we can't find the phone, you can at least look at your cell phone bill and it will give you the numbers you've called."

"Oh, good idea." Maryn ate a piece of potato, loving the buttery flavor and perfect texture. "Mama Porter is amazing. Can I take her home with me?"

Tuck shrugged. "Can we all come?" He studied her as if gauging

84

her answer. Her heart rate picked up and she wished with everything in her that she could take him home.

"Sure, but my apartment is just a bit smaller than this place." She held up her first finger and thumb about an inch apart.

Tuck laughed.

"So back to the story." Her back and head were starting to ache. Maryn knew she had a few more bites of dinner and a few more minutes of learning about Tuck before she'd have to beg for more pain pills and a ride in Tuck's arms back up to bed. At least the ride would be pleasant.

"I thought we finished the story," Tuck muttered.

"Not when you obviously haven't forgiven yourself."

Tuck set his fork down. "You know there are two types of men who want to be in the armed forces?"

"No. Explain."

"There are those who want to be the hero, save the little old lady and the children, right the wrongs of the world, and there are those who want to kill the bad guy."

She bit at her lip. "You were the hero?"

"I thought so. The psychiatrist explained that was why this was all so hard on me and Johnson. We thought we were protecting the innocents, not murdering them." His mouth drew into a thin line.

"You could claim that those innocents could grow up to be terrorists."

"You could." His dark eyes were full of misery. "Would you believe that if you pulled that trigger?"

"Probably not." Maryn felt her strength leaving her. She wanted to reassure Tuck and help him, but she had nothing left.

"I didn't either."

"Only the Lord can help you forgive yourself."

Tuck's eyebrows arched. "I didn't figure you for a believer."

"Of course I'm a believer. If I wasn't I'd be hamburger in that bear's paws."

"You kind of were hamburger."

She pushed a hand at him, but it tugged at her stitches and she cried out.

"You need to get back into bed." Tucker pushed away from the table.

"We can't leave all this food. Mama Porter would feel so bad."

"I'll come back for it. Could you eat some more if I get you upstairs and settled in the bed?"

"Maybe."

Tucker lifted Maryn into his arms and scaled the stairs. Warm tingles spread through her as she lay against his chest. He waited for her while she used the bathroom, brushed her teeth, and washed her face. Then he helped her take another pain pill and get settled comfortably in the bed.

"Where are you going to sleep?" Maryn asked groggily.

"Maybe I'll climb in there with you." His smile said he wouldn't.

"There's plenty of room." She shouldn't have said that.

Tuck sat down in the chair he'd pulled close to the bedside and leaned forward. His face was close to hers. "Don't worry about me. I can sleep anywhere."

"Good talent to have." She stared into his brown eyes, finding herself lost in them. It wasn't even dark outside and yet she was sure she could sleep for hours. "Thank you for taking such good care of me."

"You're easy to take care of."

She laughed weakly and her eyes drifted closed of their own volition. "I know that's a lie."

"It's not." She heard the leather of the recliner squeak as he leaned forward and then she felt his lips brush over hers.

Maryn's eyes popped back open. The contact had been brief, but she could still feel the impression of his lips on hers and wished she could sit up and kiss him again. "I liked that," she murmured. "A good night kiss is part of your taking care of the guest package?"

"If you weren't in pain and on drugs I'd give you a real goodnight kiss."

Maryn wished she could concentrate, but that OxyContin was hitting her hard. "I have something exhilarating to look forward to tomorrow night then."

Tucker's slow grin was the last thing she remembered as she dozed off.

Chapter Nine

Tucker hid in a cave. Sweat dripped down his face despite the fact it was much cooler in the darkened interior than outside with over a hundred degree temperatures and that blasted sun that would never stop. He was alone, but it made no sense to him. He was never alone. Johnson or one of their other troop members was always by his side.

Johnson walked into the entrance of the cave, barely enough light to see his dimples. He grinned at Tucker. "Hiding out like a wussy boy, eh?"

The ground rocked and the blast of light nearly blinded Tucker. He yelled a warning to Johnson, but as his friend's body was thrown next to him on the rocky ground, he knew it was too late.

Tuck jerked awake, panting and sweating. He looked slowly around the dark room. Snow still fell gently outside, but there was an almost ethereal light to the scene. Maryn slept soundly in the bed. She'd rolled onto her back and he wondered if he should move her, but it didn't seem to be hurting her. Braxton kept reassuring him that the cuts weren't that deep and Maryn would heal quickly. He hoped so.

Standing and shaking out his arms, he tried to shake off the dream. He had them often, and usually Johnson was killed in them. He didn't know what that meant and hoped if he and his friend were ever in danger again, Tucker could protect him. He'd actually saved Johnson's life in a scrimmage in Afghanistan, so maybe the dreams were just aftereffects of that.

Rolling his neck, he knew he needed to lie down and get a decent night's sleep. He went into his bathroom, brushed his teeth, and put on a clean t-shirt and some sweats. Walking past his bed, he told himself to go down to one of the guest bedrooms, but he didn't want to leave Maryn. He loved being around her and if she should awaken and be scared or need something, he wanted to be here.

He circled the bed and lay down on top of the covers. It felt so good to stretch out his back. Glancing over at the beautiful woman sleeping next to him, Tucker gently placed his hand over hers. He smiled to himself. He could get used to sleeping like this.

Maryn's sleep was weird. Dreams about Tuck and James fighting over her. In the background there was this scary bald dude who was following her and James. Sometimes the bear would appear and Max would be snarling and jumping at the grizzly then she'd see Tuck again like he was that night—so strong and majestic with the gun in his hands. She awakened and realized she'd rolled onto her back. "Ouch," she whispered.

"Maryn?" Tucker was not in his spot in the chair, he was in the bed right next to her. Oh, my. This could be interesting.

"Hey," she groaned. She didn't want to roll away from him so she sat up, grateful the motion didn't hurt too much. "Did I wake you?"

"No." Tucker sat up next to her. "I just laid down to... stretch my back out."

"You should be able to sleep in your own bed. I'll go down to one of the other rooms. You didn't get any sleep last night because of me and now you're hurting your back. Man, I'm an insensitive jerk."

Tucker smiled at her in the dimly lit room. Maryn's breath caught. He was a beautiful man and that rugged edge with the longish hair and huge body really did it for her. She glanced around. This was really intimate. She didn't know him that well and she'd definitely overstayed her welcome in his bed. She should go.

"I was too worried to sleep last night and I didn't want to leave you tonight in case you needed something. Do you need medicine or a drink or food? You hardly ate anything."

"I'm feeling okay," Maryn said. "Besides, what are you doing sounding like me, talking too much and too fast?"

He laughed. "I guess I feel a little awkward that I laid down by you. Would your boyfriend mind?"

Maryn scowled, wishing she hadn't said anything about that earlier. "He's not my boyfriend," she said too forcefully. "He thinks he is, but honestly I'm not committed to anyone." Silence fell for a little while and it felt stifling. "I'm sorry I've taken over your bed. I'll get out of here."

"No, please. I..." he cleared his throat. "Want you close."

Her breath caught at the honesty of his admission. She wanted him close too. For some reason, she knew she could sleep soundly with him there, and maybe the nightmares would disappear. "I need to stay on my right side. Would you mind, holding me there?" She swallowed, that had been really forward, even for her.

Tucker regarded her solemnly. "It would be a pleasure, Ms. Howe."

She smiled and laid down on her right side. He placed a pillow behind her backside. Resting her bum against it, she felt much more relaxed and grateful that he was going to keep some distance between them. Then he scooted up behind her. Tingles spread over her skin even though his body wasn't touching hers. It was close enough to feel the heat from it. He placed his hand gently on her hip to avoid the stitches. She reclined her upper body and her uninjured shoulder rested against his chest.

"Ah," she said. "This is comfy." It was so much more than comfy. She had no clue if she'd be able to sleep with all the nerves firing in her body like this. If she wasn't injured and was feeling a little more brave, she would've rolled over and kissed him.

"It is," he murmured, his breath brushing against her neck.

Maryn shivered.

"I'm sorry. Am I too close?"

"Not possible," Maryn said then bit her lip. Why did everything she think have to escape?

"Are you always this flirtatious?" Tuck's low voice rumbled across her skin again.

"Only with you," she murmured back.

Tuck's breath shortened. Maryn clamped her lips together to keep from saying anything that might make this awkward. His body next to hers was going to make it hard to sleep. She knew tomorrow she'd have to take a look at reality again, but for tonight she was going to savor his closeness.

Chapter Ten

Maryn awoke as the sky gradually lightened outside. The snow on the trees and the river was so beautiful. She felt an arm around her waist and Tucker's upper body cuddled up to hers. Inhaling, she smiled. Tuck smelled so good. She sighed and nestled a bit deeper against him. The stitches and cuts didn't hurt if she didn't move wrong and she was going to enjoy every second of his touch. When he awakened, would he want to stay close or would he be embarrassed about what had transpired last night? She'd slept peacefully and absolutely loved the way this man sheltered and protected her. Could she ever be afraid of anything with him by her side?

"Oh, my, heavens!" Mama Porter's shriek came from the doorway.

Tuck jumped in response and the movement brought the pain she'd been fearing as her body was jostled. Maryn cried out then bit her lip to try to hide the fact she was hurting. She hauled herself to a seated position and looked at Mama in the doorway and Tuck sitting up in bed next to her.

"Oh, Maryn, I hurt you. I'm sorry."

"I'm okay," she reassured him, loving that his first thought was of her.

"Tucker Shaffer! What *are* you doing?"

"Mama." Tuck looked boyish and absolutely adorable with his

hair mussed and his dark eyes unable to meet either of theirs. "I was just... taking care of her."

"I'll bet you were! And the poor dear injured like she is. Now you get out of that bed and let me help her get ready."

Tucker stood and took his lashing with a half-grin on his face.

"Don't you smile at me!" She swatted at him, but Tuck dodged it easily. "Grab your clothes and toiletries and go shower in one of the guest baths. Now, go on, get out of here."

Tucker gave her half a bow, hurried past her, and grabbed some things from his bathroom and walk-in closet. Maryn climbed out of bed, wishing she could shower too, but realizing it probably wasn't to be with all the stitches.

Tucker walked boldly to her and murmured in her ear, "No matter how mad Mama is, that was the best night's sleep I've had in a long time."

"Me too." She winked up at him.

His dark eyes shadowed by even darker lashes and his face covered in stubble made her a bit weak. She swayed and he held her elbows to steady her then escorted her into the bathroom with Mama Porter following and tsking the entire way.

"I'll see you at breakfast," he said before finally listening to Mama and heading for the stairs.

"That boy," Mama said in exasperation, but she had a twinkle in her eyes. "Did he just climb on up in bed with you?"

"Yes. But I didn't mind." Maryn had to laugh at the shock on Mama's face. "We didn't do anything inappropriate." She hastened to reassure the sweet woman. "If you noticed, he was above the covers. He simply held me so I wouldn't roll onto my back and hurt myself."

"Okay." Mama shook her head and sighed heavily. "Now, can I help you get ready?"

"I think if you'll just help me get this tank top off, I can give myself a sponge bath and get ready." Maryn sorted through the clothes in her bag, nothing comfortable or practical but the tank top and pajama bottoms. "Dang. I haven't got anything that I should probably wear with these stupid stitches."

Mama thought for a minute then bustled into the walk-in closet. She returned with a huge long-sleeved t-shirt. "This will be like a nightdress on you."

"Thank you. That will work great."

She helped Maryn pull off the tank top and pajama bottoms then left her alone. Maryn quickly washed up with a washcloth, careful not to make any sudden movements. She put on minimal makeup, re-secured her hair in the ponytail, and then picked up the t-shirt. Stretching her arms up to slide it over her head hurt, but the second the shirt slid into place, Maryn sighed. It smelled like Tuck. She rolled the sleeves. "Good choice, Mama Porter," she murmured. The woman may have acted shocked by the sleeping arrangement, but she was definitely a little matchmaker.

Maryn slowly walked out of the bathroom and down the stairs. The pain wasn't too bad today. She was going to insist on something low key like ibuprofen or Tylenol instead of OxyContin to take the edge off. She wanted to think clearly and enjoy each moment with Tucker today. Who knew how long she'd have before she had to return to real life?

As she entered the kitchen Mama, Johnson, Braxton, and Tuck all looked up. All Maryn could focus on was Tuck and the look of appreciation that filled his eyes.

"I like your shirt," he said, coming to her side and taking her elbow.

"Thanks. It smells like someone I know."

He winked and escorted her to the dining table. Maryn forced herself to break from his gaze and acknowledge the others in the room. Their mouths were slightly open and she wondered if they were all speculating on their boss's actions. "Good morning," she said.

Braxton sprang into action. "Good morning. How are you feeling today?"

"As good as peach pie. Thank you."

"I don't think peach pie ever looked that good," Johnson muttered.

Tucker shot him a dark look. Johnson grinned innocently, his dimples deepening.

"You watch that tongue," Mama Porter pointed a spatula at Johnson.

Braxton cleared his throat. "The sky is clear today so rather than check your sutures, I think we should get you into the medical center in West Yellowstone."

"Okay. After breakfast?"

"Whenever you feel up to it, ma'am."

"Thanks."

Everyone dished up their breakfast and then after a quick prayer by Johnson, they all disappeared, even Mama Porter. Tucker brought Maryn a plate loaded with pancakes, sausage, and eggs. There was no way she could eat half of it. She was hungry today though so that was good. "Could I bug you for some ibuprofen?"

Tucker jumped up. "Of course, but do you want something stronger? The doctor left Lortab if you don't want any more OxyContin."

"No thank you on either, I'm afraid I probably said enough things I shouldn't in my drug-induced coma."

Tucker grinned. "Nothing that bothered me." He rushed to a medicine cabinet and came back with a bottle of ibuprofen. Maryn took two with a swig of orange juice.

"Now why did everyone disappear?" she asked as she forked a bite of eggs. She couldn't believe how much better she felt as she sat normally in her chair, her back not fully pressed against the cushion but in contact with it.

"They all have stuff to do this morning," Tucker said.

Maryn didn't believe him for a minute, but she liked having him to herself. It was still kind of odd to her these four adults living together, but they were more like a family than she'd ever been around and all seemed to be productive and normal.

She swallowed her eggs and drizzled some strawberry syrup onto her pancake then took a bite. "Oh, these are heavenly."

"Braxton's specialty. He likes to cook breakfast."

"Nice." Maryn drank a sip of juice then asked, "So, I've heard about how you and Johnson met and Braxton was your foster grandfather that you loved and brought with you, but what's Mama Porter's story?"

Tucker chewed a bite of sausage and swallowed before saying, "It's kind of a sad story."

"I don't like those kind. Happy ending?"

"Sure, because Mama makes it happy."

"She's a sweetheart."

He ate some pancakes and then set his fork down. "Mama lost her husband and two teenaged sons in a horrible car accident. She didn't have any insurance or marketable skills so she lost her house as well. Her neighbors and church friends loved her and her next door neighbor took her in, but she always felt like a burden. She finally couldn't take it anymore so she left."

"Wait, where was this?"

"Boise, Idaho. She took a bus to Southern California and lived and cooked at a homeless shelter there. Have you heard of the Friendship Shelter?"

"Yes. It's a nicer one."

"She loved it there. Johnson and I met her while we were doing some volunteer work—painting buildings and fixing things around the place. She adopted us like we were her own and when we were ready to move to Grand Cayman, like we usually do the end of February, we forced her to come with us."

"Forced her?"

"She loved her purpose there, helping everyone. It took her mind off of things. But we make sure wherever we are to help out those around us so she gets a chance to cook and love. It's a bit harder to find opportunities here in Island Park, but sometimes I think she needs that break too."

"Wow, Tucker Shaffer. I knew you were charitably-minded, but this is a bit above and beyond. You'd love my friends Alyssa and Beck."

"What do they do?" Tuck blushed at the compliment and shoveled some pancakes in his mouth.

"Beck has a charity called Jordan's Buds that he uses to help children around the world."

"That's great. I would love to meet them someday." His eyes caught hers and held.

"I'd love for you to meet them someday... soon."

Tuck smiled at her and Maryn had to force herself to keep eating her breakfast and not climb onto his lap and see if those nice-looking lips tasted as good as she'd dreamed about from his brief kiss last night.

Chapter Eleven

After breakfast, they checked on Max again. She was rambunctious and obviously healing a lot quicker than Maryn, though Maryn really couldn't complain. She wanted to take a shower, but besides that, the pain was minimal and if she wasn't injured she wouldn't be spending all this uninterrupted time with Tucker, so there was definitely a silver lining.

They climbed all the way back upstairs and relaxed in Tucker's sitting room while they waited for Braxton and Johnson to clear the driveway so they could take Maryn to the doctor in the Range Rover instead of on a snowmobile.

"I could've ridden the snowmobile," Maryn said, sitting next to Tucker on the leather sofa. The picture was just so perfect she was gazing at—this beautiful room with the fireplace, the sun sparkling off the snow in the trees outside the window, and Tucker. She wondered if she'd ever get tired of looking at his face, which seemed to grow more handsome to her every hour, framed by his dark hair.

"I'm sure you could, but I would never do that to you."

"You just seem to want to protect me."

He reached over and squeezed her hand. "I do, plus I really like you wearing my shirt."

She blushed. "What does that have to do with anything?"

"Nothing. I just wanted to make sure you knew how good you looked in it before you change to go to the doctor."

Maryn couldn't help but smile. "Thank you." She leaned against the left side of the comfortable leather sofa and savored his hand holding hers and the warmth of the fire. "I wish I could just stay here all day."

"You could. UPS delivered a huge shipment of books the day before you came. We could read together and sit by the fire."

Maryn loved the image he was painting.

He exhaled slowly. "But we did promise the doctor we'd bring you in today and I want to make sure you heal properly." His voice dropped. "Can't stand the thought of scars on that beautiful back."

Maryn hadn't even thought about scarring. The cuts were low enough if the scars didn't fade very few people would ever see them except for maybe in a swimsuit. She wondered what her husband would think of the scars someday. She studied Tucker as that thought rolled around in her head.

He returned her gaze and gave her a smile that had her sweating. Maybe they should turn the fireplace off. He dropped his gaze and cleared his throat. "I forgot to tell you, Johnson found the paperwork for your rental when he cleaned out your car for you. He got a hold of them this morning and they'll come soon and take care of the car. The rental's insurance will cover everything."

Maryn smiled at him. "Thank you. That's nice to not worry about. So what do we do *after* we visit the doc and read to our heart's content by the fireplace?" Maryn looked at him from beneath lowered lashes. She should've been back in California by now. She needed to go home and write Tucker's story, which she now had plenty of information for, but for the first time in her adult life the story wasn't the motivation. There was something about this house, these people, and especially Tuck that made her reluctant to leave. Crazy that a couple of days ago she'd run for her life and now she had no desire to leave.

"Well." Tuck smiled at her. "I'm hoping we could talk you into staying with us for a few more days. You wouldn't want to make me drive in all this snow to the airport." He winked.

She smiled, certain driving in the snow didn't bother him and thrilled that he was willing to drive her to the airport when that time came. "No, I wouldn't want to do that." She met his gaze and made sure he knew through her look exactly why she wanted more time with him.

Tucker scooted a bit closer and wrapped his arm around her shoulder. "Maryn?" his voice dropped low and husky.

"Yes?" she gazed up at him and moistened her lips.

His head slowly descended toward hers. Maryn was transfixed by the smoldering look in those dark eyes.

The doorbell rang and seconds later the front door banged open and shouting could be heard from the foyer.

Tucker jumped to his feet, looking back at Maryn. "Stay here, please."

Maryn nodded. Whatever was going on, she was in no condition to get in the middle of what sounded like a brawl. Footsteps pounded up the grand staircase.

"Where are you keeping her?" someone yelled.

Maryn stood too quickly, wincing at the tug to her stitches. "James?" she whispered.

"She's upstairs," Mama said, "but you can't just go up there."

Tuck turned back to her. His brow wrinkling and his jaw set. "James?" he asked.

Maryn shook her head and walked to Tuck's side. "Let me talk to him. He'll listen to me."

James stormed into the sitting room, literally dragging Braxton behind him. James shook off the elderly man and slammed a fist into Tuck's face. Tuck hardly flinched from the blow.

100

"How dare you kidnap her?" James screamed, swinging at Tuck again. Tuck was prepared this time and grabbed James' arm and held it tight.

"James! You overprotective idiot!" Maryn snapped at James, wishing she felt good enough to smack him. "He didn't kidnap me."

"Sorry," Braxton said to Tucker. "We had the gate open removing the snow and they came through."

"It's okay," Tuck muttered.

James' gaze swept over Maryn, wearing only Tuck's over-sized T-shirt and some socks. "Oh. I see how it is." He wrenched his arm free and backed up several steps. "Always acting like the pure little woman, but all along you've been holding out for the billionaire like your stupid friends."

Maryn flinched like he'd slapped her. James had never spoken to her like that and always reassured her that he respected her desire to wait for marriage.

Tuck took a menacing step forward. "You need to apologize. Maryn has done nothing wrong."

James sneered at him, but took a large step backward.

Maryn walked to Tuck's side and took his hand in hers. She felt a fierce sense of protection for Tucker and wanted to show James whose side she was on. "I was attacked by a grizzly, you jerk, and Tuck not only saved me but has been taking care of me the past two days."

"I'll bet he has." James rolled his eyes.

"You had better back up," Maryn said. "Tuck has been nothing but a gentleman." She glanced at Tucker. The look in his eyes was one of protection and jealousy. He wanted her and she loved it. Her face flared as she remembered Tucker climbing into bed with her last night. So *something* had happened, but not what James was suggesting. "What are you even doing here James? We sent messages to the magazine that I was fine."

"Like I'd believe some cryptic message from his crony." James huffed and folded his arms across his chest. "You haven't answered a call or text in two days. I've been really worried about you."

Maryn bit at her lip. She should've found some time to call him back after she hung up on him and reassure him that the interview was going well, but she was too absorbed with Tuck and then everything happened. It wasn't her fault that James had assumed the worst and reacted like this, but she did appreciate that James worried about her and was trying in his own way to show it.

"I've got a camera crew here and made sure to inform a lot of people that I am here rescuing Maryn from you," he directed at Tucker, "so you'd better not try anything if you don't want your stock to plummet."

Any appreciation flew out the window. "Rescuing? Really James. Tuck is the one who rescued me." James was just trying to get attention for his beloved magazine. Big surprise.

"I don't care about my stock," Tuck growled. "You're going to apologize to Maryn for your insinuations then you're going to get off my property."

"Not without Maryn."

"She's not leaving with you." Tuck stood so strong and bold, but James wasn't backing down. There was going to be a battle if she didn't do something about it. Obviously, Tuck would win that battle, but James would resort to ugly tactics. He'd use that camera crew to exploit Tuck and his friends and she couldn't allow that. She glanced up at this tough man who had been through so much and knew she'd do anything to protect him, even if that meant leaving him.

"I'll go," Maryn interrupted.

Tuck swung to face her and the pain in his eyes about buckled her knees.

James spread his hands wide and grinned. "That's my girl."

Maryn ignored James' comment, watching Tucker's fists clench.

"I need to get back to work, to my real life," she tried to explain to Tucker. "Being here with you has been..." She looked over his shoulder at James. "Can you please wait for me outside? I need to change my clothes and say goodbye."

"As long as he doesn't help you change your clothes," James muttered.

"Go!" Tuck commanded.

James brushed a lock of blond hair from his face and slowly turned and walked down the stairs. Braxton gave him an imperious glare and followed. Maryn couldn't believe the way James was acting. He obviously thought he was coming to her rescue, but to bring a camera crew? That was slimy.

Tuck stood with the muscles in his shoulders bunched into knots, not looking at her.

"Thank you," Maryn said.

"For what?" he muttered.

Maryn moved to within inches of his chest. She reached up and gently turned his chin until he was looking at her. "Thank you for saving me from the bear and thank you for the past three days. They've been the most... relaxing time of my life, no relaxing isn't quite the right word." Especially when she thought about snuggling him throughout the night. "Stress free." She shook her head. "No, that isn't it either." Tuck had stressed her quite a bit until she'd seen into his heart. "Enjoyable. Yes, even though I could've done without the bear attack and the stitches, being with you has been wonderful."

Tuck simply watched her during her monologue. He reached up and captured her hand, drew it to his mouth and kissed her palm. Her heartrate increased as his dark eyes bore into her. "Then why are you leaving?"

Maryn looked down, unable to hold that gaze. "I have a life, Tuck. I need to write and be with..." She about said my friends, but with Alyssa married and busy, her exercise, church, and work friends were fun, but they weren't close friends who needed her. James was about the only friend who seemed to need her, and at the moment she couldn't imagine wanting to spend time with him.

"That James guy?" Tuck scowled.

"No. I just... can't stay." She wanted him to beg her to stay and be part of his life. She could write from here. They could make it work. She shook her head. It had only been three days since she met him. You don't make that kind of commitment after three days, one brief kiss when you're on drugs, and a night of snuggling. It was ridiculous. She looked over Tuck's broad frame, his large hands that could be so tender, those dark eyes she could get lost in, those lips... Three days wasn't nearly long enough.

"James will make a scene and make you look bad," she murmured.

"I don't care what the media thinks of me." His eyes begged her to believe him.

"I know, but I do." Maryn placed a hand on his chest, feeling his strong muscles under her palm. "It's better this way. Believe me. James is... very convincing when he wants to be and he'll shred both of our lives." She'd been convinced that James was a good person, but right now she was doubting that.

Tucker's broad shoulders rounded. He took a step closer to her, reaching up and cupping her cheek with his hand. "If it's better for you, I'll let you go. If you promise to stop by the Instacare in Rexburg or Idaho Falls before you fly out."

She nodded, grateful he cared so much.

Tucker exhaled slowly then gave her a soft smile. "Have I told you I really like you in my shirt?"

"Why Tucker Shaffer, you're sounding a bit possessive." Maryn batted her eyelashes, but could hardly catch her breath with him standing so close and looking at her like that.

"More than a bit." His hand trailed along her jaw and into her hair. "I love the way you say my name," his voice was low and oh so appetizing.

"I love saying it." She paused then asked, "Do you know the worst part about leaving?" Biting at her lip, she hoped he wouldn't think her too forward.

"What's that?" His breath was coming in short puffs as he bent his head closer to hers.

"Last night you promised me a better good night kiss tonight and now I won't be here to make you keep your promise."

Tucker smiled and she got distracted by that scar at the corner of his mouth. She reached up and traced it with her finger then went on tiptoes and kissed the scar. Tucker turned his head and she gasped at the intensity in his eyes. He brushed his lips across hers and she sighed from the sweetness of it.

Tucker took her face in both of his large hands and gave her a kiss for the record books. Maryn clung to his shoulders as he manipulated her mouth with a soft passion that fit him—strong, caring, and thorough. He slowed down the kiss and gently ran his hands along her arms until he grasped her hands then rested his forehead against hers. "Was that a bit better than last night?"

Maryn blinked as if waking from a deep sleep. "I'm not even sure where I am at this moment."

Tucker chuckled and tenderly kissed her again. "I guess that will have to last you until I see you again."

"Will I... see you again?"

"A bear couldn't keep me away."

Maryn shuddered and Tucker grimaced. "Sorry, bad joke."

"No. The image of you protecting me from that bear is something I never want to forget." She sighed and pulled away. "I'd better get going."

He nodded and released her hands.

She turned, walked back into his bathroom, and softly shut the door. Her overnight bag was in the closet. Slipping his shirt off, she shoved it in her bag. It was painful, but she managed to get back into her own clothes, run a brush through her hair and put on some powder, mascara, and lipstick. James had cameras outside. Man, she was ticked at him right now. She had no desire to write any kind of article about Tuck. James had acted like he brought the cameras to rescue her, but it was for profit, she knew that as well as she knew that she didn't want to leave Tucker Shaffer. Ever.

She shouldered her bag and her purse that she'd all but forgotten about, Braxton had brought it to her this morning. Apparently she'd left it in the office when she ran from Tucker first night. She opened the door. Tuck still stood in the sitting room, his shoulders slightly hunched and an unreadable expression on his face. He turned and offered a sad smile. "It was a pleasure to meet you, Maryn Howe."

"The pleasure was mine, Tucker Shaffer. Please know that I will only reveal the best things about you."

He crossed the room to her in three long strides, not touching her, but so close she could feel his breath on her forehead. "What are the best things about me?"

She glanced up and met his eyes. "All of you."

Tuck wrapped his arms carefully around her back, avoiding her injuries, lowered his head and kissed her until she couldn't tell which way was up. The kiss was full of heated passion, but also surprisingly innocent and pure.

Releasing her, he backed up a couple of steps and murmured, "I'll miss you."

Maryn about broke then and begged him to let her stay. "Don't forget me," she whispered.

"Not possible."

She clutched her bags with trembling hands and forced herself to turn from his brown eyes that were looking so mournful and sad at her and place one foot in front of the other. Somehow she made it down all the stairs without tripping and falling. Johnson, Braxton, and Mama Porter all stood in the entryway, glaring at James, who was tapping away on his phone, acting oblivious to the undercurrent. Her heart softened a fraction. James always pulled out his phone when he was nervous. This was an awkward situation for him and she knew in his twisted way he did think he was rescuing her.

Mama Porter broke from the stoic group of three and rushed to her. She hugged her gently. "Darling, girl. Are you sure you can't stay?"

Maryn nodded bravely. She felt Tuck's eyes on her and looked up the three stories to see him next to the railing, his dark eyes so full of sadness. She lifted her fingers, kissed them, and pushed them his direction. He smiled.

Forcing herself to focus on Mama Porter, she said, "Thank you for everything, I hope to come see all of you again, some day, real soon, that is when you're not snowed in and I don't have to drive a snowmobile to get in here."

"As soon as you can, dear." Mama Porter squeezed her hand, then stepped away, wiping at her eyes with a handkerchief.

Braxton shook Maryn's hand with all seriousness. "It was a pleasure to meet you, Ms. Howe."

Him saying pleasure like that had her glancing up at Tuck again, but he was gone. She bit her lip to keep in the cry of pain. "Thank you, Braxton."

"Will you promise to go to the Instacare before you fly out and then visit with your doctor at home tomorrow?"

"I will. Thank you for stitching me up."

He nodded formally.

Johnson came next, giving her a brotherly side hug. "I've never seen the big guy like this," he whispered in her ear. "Please, keep in touch and don't make any asinine decisions." He glared at James who had finally pocketed his phone and was watching them all warily.

"Good advice, mate," she whispered back and squeezed his arm. He released her and James was immediately there, wrapping his arm around her back. "Ouch," she cried out.

"Oh, sorry, I don't know where you're hurt at."

"Don't touch my lower back or left side," she said, thinking of how perfectly Tuck had managed to touch her without hurting any of the wounds moments before.

James took her overnight bag and then held her arm and escorted her to the front door. Maryn tugged him to a stop. "Please tell them not to shoot this."

"You can do this, Mar. Come on, I'm right here with you." He beamed at her. "Your story is going to be the biggest hit of the year. We'll use this video footage on all our social media and splash his name all over it, pointing them to the article you're going to write

about him. You can say whatever you like. It's going to be amazing."
He swung the door open and sure enough there were videographers
and photographers, some staff from the magazine who called out
greetings to her.

Maryn gritted her teeth, forced a smile, and allowed James to
escort her down the stairs. She only allowed herself to look back
once. Mama Porter, Braxton, and Johnson all watched from the
porch steps and if she glanced way up she could see the dark eyes of
the man she'd fallen in serious like with the past three days,
watching her being taken away by jerk-bait James.

Chapter Twelve

The next two weeks dragged like a kayak trying to pull a water skier through the ocean. James had taken Maryn to an Instacare in Idaho Falls before they flew out. They'd done a thorough exam including an MRI to make sure she had no damage that'd been missed, checked her sutures, and gave her some Lortab for the trip home. She'd endured the airplane ride and been thankful that the drugs made her sleepy and cut the pain enough that it was all a blur.

The next day she drove herself into the doctor because James was too busy marketing Tucker Shaffer's story. He claimed he was fulfilling their dreams to have The Rising Star top the charts for circulation, but those weren't her dreams anymore. She'd left a lot of her dreams in Island Park when she realized there was more to life than writing and being recognized for her writing. Tuck was what she dreamed about now.

The doctor was impressed with how well done the stitches were and gave her some cream that he promised would minimize any scarring. It was a relief a week later when the stitches were removed. The nurse helped her look at all of the markings on her back in the mirror and she was impressed with Braxton's skills as well.

She poured herself into the article on Tucker, reliving every wonderful minute she'd spent with him as she wrote, shivering as she remembered the bear attack, smiling to herself as she thought of something sweet Tucker had said. She was having trouble sleeping at night and wished he was there to hold her. Wearing his shirt helped, but the smell faded and then she ached for him all the more.

As soon as she got a new phone she texted Tucker. He immediately texted back and the highlight of her day came when he started texting her every night. They shared funny things that had happened throughout their days and sometimes it dipped into flirtation, but neither of them approached the subject of when they'd see each other again. She missed his voice and wanted to call him, but there was a gulf between them and she knew it was her fault. She was the one who'd allowed James to take her away from him.

The article consumed her. It would've been twenty pages long if she had her way, but she eventually found a way to cut three-quarters of what she wrote before finally passing it off to editing. James was impatient for the final product, but she wanted to make sure she didn't reveal anything that would hurt Tuck or his friends.

Many hours were spent looking through the pictures Johnson had emailed to her. He'd done a great job capturing the exact poses and locations she'd requested. Less time could've been taken selecting the best shots for the article, but Maryn found herself sighing and drooling over picture after picture of Tucker. He'd been extremely attractive when she first met him, but the longer she'd spent with him the more his appeal grew. She studied the strong planes of his face, his longish dark hair, those intriguing brown eyes, and those lips she wished she could feel on hers again, for so long that she feared she would grow cross-eyed. If only she could see him again in person.

Almost hourly she entertained happy thoughts about packing up her Bug and driving to Island Park. The image of Johnson opening the gate to her and then Tucker waiting for her on the porch always got her heart thumping. Then she talked herself into reality. Her life was in L.A. She looked around her little apartment and wondered about that life. It certainly seemed empty lately. Alyssa and Beck were due back from Honduras tomorrow. That would help, but they were so in love it was sometimes hard to be around them, be a spectator to their fulfilling life. Maryn was simply a fun friend to go to lunch with on occasion. She'd gone roller-blading and to movies with her church friends and been texting a couple of her girl's camp friends, Haley and MacKenzie more, trying to convince one of them to come visit, but they both had busy lives of their own.

James was acting really weird and he was driving her crazy. He begged her to come into the office more, he asked her to lunch and dinner every day, and he couldn't stop pledging his love to her, even though she tried time and again to explain she didn't feel the same. It was over the top. She recognized she'd changed too, but it was like her former friend was trying too hard, pretending to be something he wasn't.

James had been a good friend to her, but her feelings for him were nothing compared to Tucker. James' career and them achieving notoriety together used to be their goals. Now it seemed like making money had become James' sole motivation. If she was honest, she used to care about her career with that same intensity. Now she wasn't sure what she wanted out of life... except a chance to be with Tucker more.

Two weeks after the accident, the article was done and set to print the next day. James had finally talked her into going out to dinner. She was lonely and the article was a reason to celebrate. She hoped Tuck would love it.

While she waited for James to arrive, she picked up her phone and saw she had a text from Tucker.

Hey, I noticed one of my favorite shirts has disappeared.

Oh? I wonder what happened to it.

I'm just hoping the girl who stole it will send me a picture with her in it.

Maryn bit at her lip and grinned. It was much easier to text brave words so she plunged ahead, *Maybe you should come see it for yourself. It looks better in person.*

There was a pause, too long of a pause for her to feel comfortable. A knock came at the door. She stood reluctantly, wanting to see Tuck's answer. As she walked to the door, her phone chimed.

Maybe I will.

Maryn held the phone to her chest, smiling.

James drove them to Otium, a contemporary restaurant near the cultural corridor of Grand Avenue. She'd dressed in a long, sleeveless black dress that was comfortable and classy with a red wrap around her shoulders and red and black striped heels.

James gunned into the parking lot, squealing the brakes. He grinned over at Maryn and rubbed his hand across the dash. "Do you like it?"

"What happened to your Altima?"

James scoffed. "Upgraded. It's a Maserati, Mar!" He looked like a little boy with his first homemade go-kart, but Maryn knew enough about cars to know there was nothing homemade about a Maserati.

The valet opened Maryn's door and she stepped out, biting her tongue when she wanted to ask James why he would go into debt for a flashy car. Had he gotten a raise she hadn't heard about?

"Can we eat outside?" Maryn asked as James took her elbow and escorted her into the restaurant.

"Of course. Anything you want. You are so beautiful tonight. Did I tell you that?"

Maryn didn't reciprocate. James was handsome in his suit, but she knew he highlighted his hair, and his nails were definitely manicured. Tucker would never highlight and the thought of him sitting through a manicure was hilarious. She smiled to herself. James grinned in return, assuming she was smiling at him.

The maître d' led them to a table out on the patio and Maryn was happy to enjoy the warm night air. That was one benefit of southern California over Island Park. It was warm outside most of the year. She held in a sigh. Island Park had better perks than weather. It had Tucker Shaffer.

Maryn declined the wine list. James ordered them a Cabernet from Italy. She sipped her water as he tilted his head to the side. "Why don't you ever drink with me?"

She smiled. "I need to keep my wits about me when I'm with you."

"Because I'm so irresistible?"

"Keep telling yourself that." They used to have such fun banter and Maryn missed their lighthearted friendship.

He winked. "You should be very proud, Maryn. Everyone is clamoring for that article tomorrow. It will be the highest distribution we've ever had."

Maryn shrugged. "You did a good job of promoting it." She tried to keep the venom out of her voice, but James had splayed her picture and the story of the bear attack all over the place. He'd made Tucker look like a hero, which she appreciated, but she knew it was to sell magazines and get more advertising dollars because he definitely didn't like Tucker.

James' phone beeped. He pulled it out, read the text, and frowned. "I apologize, Mar. Can you excuse me for a minute?"

"If I must."

He chuckled and patted her hand.

She glanced over her menu, debating between the salmon and the scallops as she waited for James. She heard his voice out on the street. "I need you to bring my car up for a minute, I forgot something."

"I could retrieve whatever you need," the valet said.

"No. I need to get it myself."

"Of course, sir."

Maryn sat up straighter. Please say James wasn't getting a ring or some kind of present for her. He'd proposed more times than she could count, but she'd always been able to laugh him off as he'd never done the formal get down on his knee or anything. Her palms started sweating. She sat still and listened until she heard James thanking the valet. Slipping out of her chair, she passed their waitress on her way through the restaurant.

"Is everything all right, miss?" the waitress asked.

Maryn wondered how pale her face was. "Oh, yes." She waved a hand. "If my date returns will you please tell him I went to the restroom?"

"Of course."

Maryn slipped out the restaurant door in time to see James lift a small present from his trunk then give the valet some cash and stride off around the back of the restaurant. Weird. If the present was for her, wouldn't he be bringing it back inside? She should feel relief, but something was off.

She quietly followed him, not sure what her excuse would be if he caught her, but it was James. He wouldn't care. He usually shared everything with her. Yet for some reason, she didn't want him to see her.

Low voices reached her as she paused at the edge of the building. Peeking her head around, she saw James and two really rough-looking dudes—tats, shaggy heads, and scruffy clothes—at the back of the alley. James handed over the package and the guy gave him an envelope. What in the ecosphere was going on? At least she didn't have to worry about the present being for her.

One of the guys lifted his head and stared right at her. Maryn scurried around the side of the building, flattening herself against the wall.

"What?" James said.

"Some blonde chick was spying on us."

Maryn took off at a run. She had to make it back into the restaurant before they saw her. Her heels slowed her down. Oh, crap, they were going to catch her. A service entrance was to her right. Not stopping to think, she jerked it open and then slowly closed it. Leaning against it, she heard footsteps pounding past. She turned around and swallowed hard. The entire kitchen staff was watching her.

Patting her hair, she gave them a smile and walked straight through. "Is this the way to the restroom?"

"Um, yes, ma'am," a chef with a starched apron and white chef's hat said to her.

"Everything smells fabulous," she said and waved a hand like she knew what she was doing. "Carry on."

Ignoring the whispers and stares, Maryn hurried through the kitchen and out into the restaurant. Trying to get her ragged breathing under control, she slowed her steps and prayed the sweat dripping down her neck and chest wasn't visible.

Finally, she reached their table, sank into her seat, and took a long drink of water, using her napkin to dab at the moisture on her forehead. Her heartbeat wouldn't slow down, but she thought she looked under control when James reappeared a few minutes later.

She arched an eyebrow. "Everything okay?"

"What do you mean?" He stared at her like he knew she'd spied on him.

"You were gone for a while."

"Sorry. Just had to meet with a source about a story." He held up a hand and pumped his eyebrows. "Nope, not sharing the scoop. It's a good one and you'd try to steal it out from under me."

"Come on, I've never done that." Maryn laughed, exhaling in relief. Oh, thank heavens. James wasn't involved in some nefarious plot. Everything made sense now. Those scary guys were the source. He'd given them a gift and they'd given him some information. She almost confided that she'd watched, but something in her gut still felt uneasy.

"You have done that." James pointed an accusatory finger at her. "And probably still will, even though you're going to be famous in your own right after tomorrow."

Maryn forced a smile at him, grateful when the waitress appeared. She used to be so driven about her career, but for some reason it didn't matter as much to her anymore. Okay, she knew the reason and it was currently nine hundred and seventy eight miles away. She really needed to stop asking Siri that distance.

Chapter Thirteen

Tucker tried to keep himself busy, but it didn't work. It didn't come close to working. He thought about Maryn nonstop, but he still couldn't stand the fact that she'd left. If she cared for him and wanted to be with him, why had she left with that James guy and why hadn't she come back?

He marched into his office and clicked his mouse. Maybe some time spent programming could distract him. He'd used physical exertion to divert himself many times before, but it wasn't doing a thing for him right now. No matter how hard he ran, boxed, lifted weights, chopped wood, or cleared dead trees out of his forest, he could still think, and when he thought, it was about the blonde beauty who had walked out his front door on the arm of a fake pretty boy loser. The guy dressed like a flamer, punched about as hard as Mama when she caught Tuck sneaking cookie dough, and looked like his hair was highlighted. Tucker rolled his eyes. If that was Maryn's semi-boyfriend then Tucker definitely wasn't her type. That thought made him even more grumpy.

Next to his computer was a magazine... with a picture of him, Mama Porter, Braxton, and Johnson on the front page. *The Rising Star.* His breath caught. He wondered who had snuck it in. He knew the article was supposed to come out this week, they'd hyped it so much on social media he would've had to be a hermit without the internet to not know. Maryn had emailed him to approve the article, but he'd told her he trusted her and whatever she printed was fine with him. It didn't really matter to him how the public perceived him, no matter what his PR people stressed about. He'd told Sylvia, his PR contact yesterday to just deal with Johnson from now on. He was done worrying about that kind of bunk and Johnson didn't mind it. Yet, he was still terrified of how Maryn truly perceived him.

He swallowed hard and picked up the glossy magazine. Slowly, he turned the pages until he saw the spread. Lots of pictures of him, his friends, and his house. Johnson had taken those pictures and Tuck had tried to pose and look happy. It had been torture. He scanned the entire article but there were no pictures of Maryn. He breathed a sigh of relief. He didn't like how that James guy had exploited her to advertise the article. He considered threatening the guy with a lawsuit or better yet a boxing match, but he kept reminding himself that Maryn was a big girl and could stand up for herself if she wanted to.

Leaning back in his office chair, he started reading.

The first impression I had of Tucker Shaffer was to wonder why in Hades a fine-looking, charismatic, and well-spoken man would hide away from the world. As I learned his story, I realized he has every right to stay hidden and it's the world who is missing out.

Tucker grinned. He devoured the article, gratitude for that feisty blonde and an even stronger craving to be with her accompanied him. She painted him in much too kind of light, sharing a bit about his history and the way he developed Friend Zone and how Johnson helped it take off. She told about the feelings of warmth and friendship in his house. How he'd taken in these people, and though at first she thought they were kind of an odd bunch, four adults living the life of recluses together, they were one of the most amazing family units she'd ever been around. The article went on sharing how generous he was and all they each did to help others.

Tuck sat the magazine down and gazed out the window. The snow had almost melted over the past few weeks and everything looked fresh outside, the green boughs of the pine trees sparkling in the sun. Another storm would bring more snow, but he wondered if he'd be here to see it. He needed Maryn. Two weeks apart had done nothing to detox him from craving her laugh, her touch, her funny expressions. The only cure was Maryn. What was he doing giving James unlimited access to her and not fighting for his chance?

He stood and strode into the living room. Johnson, Braxton, and Mama were all there talking. "What do you think if we pack some clothes and fly to California?"

Mama whooped and clapped her hands together. Braxton gave him a knowing smile. Johnson muttered, "Finally pulled your head out."

Tucker grinned and turned on his heel.

"Where are you going?" Mama Porter asked.

"To pack."

She giggled and he couldn't help laughing at himself. Now that the decision was made he couldn't get to Maryn fast enough.

Chapter Fourteen

Maryn dried off from the shower and threw on an old t-shirt and jogging shorts. She'd driven to the beach and gone for a run earlier tonight. Her own treat for the article's success and it had been a huge success. Highest circulation in the history of the magazine. James told her she was getting a bonus. He tried to talk her into dinner again but she begged off, claiming she was tired.

She checked her phone one more time, hoping for another text from Tuck. The texts helped, but weren't enough to satiate her craving for Tucker Shaffer. Not even close to enough. She missed him, Mama Porter, Braxton, and Johnson, but especially she missed him. When would she see him again? She hadn't asked if he'd read the article, but hoped he liked it if he had.

Her doorbell rang. Wet hair and not a stitch of makeup. Oh, well, it was probably just James. He claimed he loved her so he'd better not be bugged by seeing her au naturale. Tuck had seen her looking absolutely horrible, banged up and makeup running down her face and he'd told her she was beautiful and taken the sweetest care of her. Dang she missed him and wished their goodbye kiss hadn't been a one and done kind of kiss.

Glancing through the peephole, her legs trembled and she braced herself against the doorframe. "Tuck," she whispered. Even distorted by the peephole, he looked amazing. She swung the door open wide and just stared. His dark hair seemed a bit longer, but still had that amazing curl. His large frame filled out a pair of jeans and short-sleeved button down shirt in a way only Tuck could do. Those chocolate brown eyes were warm and fastened on her face.

Maryn ran a hand through her hair and bit her lip. "Hey," she managed. Her mouth was dry. All words were gone. All she could think about was the last time she'd seen him and that kiss. Had he missed her as much as she'd missed him?

"Maryn." He gave her a ghost of a smile. "I'm sorry, I didn't call before, but I wanted to surprise you and..." His eyes swept over her then he crossed the threshold in one large step and pulled her fiercely against him. His mouth covered hers with a possessiveness and fire that was all Tuck. He pulled back much too soon, dropping his arms to his side. "I'm sorry... I missed you."

"No, it's fine, it's great." It was better than great. Why had he pulled back? She self-consciously pushed her wet hair out of her face. "Do you want to come in?" *And keep kissing me, please.*

Tuck shook his head quickly. "I shouldn't."

Maryn felt a pang. Despite the kiss, there was an awkwardness between them. Didn't he want to be alone with her? Why was he here and why had he kissed her like that? Just to elevate her hopes and then crush them? That was so cruel.

"I, um, wanted to ask you on a date."

"A date?" She stared at him with her mouth open. *Come on, girl, you know what a date is!*

"Yes." He shuffled his feet and glanced past her. "But I understand if you don't have... time."

"Oh, I have time. Freelance writer, remember? I can work anytime I want. In fact, I do, work anytime I want, sometimes four a.m. if I can't sleep and it's too dark to go for a run and the stinking gym doesn't open until five even though I've begged and offered to pay extra…" She trailed off. "Sorry, I'm rambling. I'd love to go on a date with you."

His slow grin had appeared during her monologue. When she finally stopped talking, he turned serious again. "Tomorrow at eight a.m.?"

Whoa. She was not a morning girl, despite her desire to have the gym open at four. That was only when she couldn't sleep for all the ideas percolating in her head or when she was missing Tuck so horribly sleep wouldn't come. Usually, she fell asleep around two a.m. and woke after nine. "Sure. Eight sounds perfect."

"I'll see you then." He smiled again and turned on his heel.

"Tuck!"

He looked back over his shoulder.

"I'm… glad you're here."

Studying her for a second, his smile made that scar appear at the corner of his mouth and her knees quivered. "Me too," he said. "See you in the morning."

She watched him walk away and pressed a hand to her heart. Tuck was taking her on a date. Screaming, she did a little dance and then ran back into her apartment. She was going to work her tail off tonight so tomorrow she could be completely free.

Her phone rang. She looked at the name. James. Hmm. Ignore it or deal with him? She forced herself to press the green button. "Hey."

"Hey, you. Sure you don't want to go out tonight? I'm on cloud seventeen here. You rocked that article, love. I have no idea how you can be tired. I'm living on adrenaline."

Maryn smiled. She did appreciate his enthusiasm. "I'm glad, James. It's been a great day." She thought of the reason for her great day and the way Tuck had looked. Why hadn't she attacked him?

Was it going to be awkward between them for a while? They'd gotten so close in those three days, she never thought it would change but now it was like they were starting all over again with him asking her on a date and why couldn't they just skip back to the familiarity and nonstop kissing? Definitely needed the kissing. But at least he was here. He'd come here, to southern California. She hadn't even asked him why. To be with her? Oh, my, she hoped so.

"Maryn? Maryn?"

"Oh, excuse me, James. Did you ask me something?" She walked into her kitchen and pulled out a pan, filling it with water. Noodles and marinara would have to do for dinner tonight.

"Only about twenty somethings." He chuckled. "Hey, I get it. You're so happy you're exhausted. Go to bed early or better yet go get a massage or mani-pedi."

Maryn smirked. Tuck would probably have no clue what a mani-pedi was and she liked that. "Okay. Thanks for understanding."

"But tomorrow I'm not taking no for an answer. I've got a reservation at Perch."

Oh, man. What excuse now? And Perch. Yikes. That was fancy and romantic. She really needed to break James' heart. It was so hard with the friendship they'd developed and their working relationship as well. He'd been a solid friend for her the past few years.

"I can't tomorrow. How about Friday instead?"

"Why?"

"Alyssa gets home tomorrow. I want to spend the day with her and Beck." She stared into the water that wasn't boiling and swallowed hard.

"And I can't come along? I love Alyssa and I'd like to meet Beck again. What a great interview those two would be."

"You're not interviewing them."

"I know, but you got to admit it would be a good one."

Maryn agreed, but she would protect her friends' privacy. She hated herself for lying to James. She couldn't do this to one of the few longtime friends she had. "James. I lied."

"What? The Maryn I know isn't capable of lying. The truth just shoots out of her beautiful mouth. Sometimes too much truth."

She exhaled loudly. "I know. I'm sorry. I didn't know how to tell you."

"What?"

The water finally popped a few bubbles and Maryn poured in some farfalle noodles.

"What's going on Mar? You in trouble? I can help. You know I'm here for you."

"I know that James." Oh, she was a jerk. She poked at the noodles and finally let it spill out. "Tucker stopped by tonight and asked me on a date."

"Tucker Shaffer?" She couldn't tell if James sounded more hurt or incredulous.

"Yes."

"What is *he* doing in town? I thought you said in your article that he always followed some schedule like a robot. He's a weirdo, Mar. I know he was good to you, but you need to be careful."

Maryn prickled as she jammed the fork at the noodles. "He's an amazing man, James. I'd suggest you lay off bagging on him."

"O-kay. So what are you doing on your date?" There was a definite sneer coming through the line now.

"I don't know. He's picking me up at eight."

"Kind of late."

"In the morning."

"What! Are you spending the night with him again? Don't give me your bull, Maryn. You slept with him, didn't you?" His voice was so full of rage she could feel it through the phone line.

Maryn gasped and clenched the phone until her knuckles turned white, and then she hung up on him.

She poked furiously at the noodles then opened a bottle of marinara sauce and poured a quarter of it into a saucepan. "Stupid idiot. He has no right. I hate him so much!"

The phone rang and she ignored it. After five more times of it ringing she put it on silent and finished assembling her simple dinner. She was too angry to eat though. A pounding on the door made her jump. She ran to it, hoping Tucker had returned. No such luck. James.

"Let me in, Mar. I know you're here."

She leaned against the door and said nothing.

"I'm sorry, okay. I just get insanely jealous when I think of you with someone else, especially him."

"Why especially him?" she asked through the door.

"He's wealthy and mysterious and he saved you from a bear. Who does that? How can I compete with that?"

Maryn wanted to tell him he couldn't compete, but she just wasn't able to force the words out. She opened the door partway. James' hair was ruffled and his perfectly pressed shirt was untucked and halfway unbuttoned.

"Hey," he whispered. "I'm sorry." He reached out a hand and trailed it down her cheek.

Maryn used to wish she felt any kind of sparks from his touch, but it was like a longtime friend or brother and now that she'd experienced Tucker's touch she understood James couldn't compete. "It's okay."

"I hate this jealousy, Mar. Please tell me you still... have feelings for me."

"I don't know James, I want to give him a chance." Dangit! Why was she being such a wimp? She needed to end this now, but she knew it would be the end of their longtime friendship and work was going to be a mess with the awkwardness.

He hung his head. "I understand, but can you at least give me another date? See how it goes with him tomorrow and give him his chance, but save Friday night for me?"

Maryn felt awful for him. He'd been there for her through so many different things and she really did like the guy, he was a great friend. But he was right, Tuck had saved her from a bear and stolen her heart. How did someone compete with that?

"Okay."

James straightened up, grabbed her, and kissed her before she could jerk away. It was quick and didn't do much for her, but it made him grin. "Thank you, Mar. I'll pick you up Friday at six."

He strode away from her apartment toward his low slung sports car. Maryn still hadn't asked him how much the monthly payments were on that puppy. Not that it was her business, but it seemed silly to drive a car that spendy when you couldn't afford it.

He lifted a hand to her, grinning like she'd been watching him go because she was pining over him or something. Maryn closed the door and sighed. Friday night she'd have to be her blunt self and explain that they were done dating. Her thoughts immediately strayed to Tucker and their date tomorrow. She was going to eat dinner now and somehow go to bed early tonight. If she had to she'd take a sleeping pill or a lavender bath and melatonin. She was going to be well-rested and ready for whatever Tucker had planned tomorrow. Her excitement over the date was so high she knew she'd need several sleeping pills to get any sleep tonight.

Chapter Fifteen

The boat cut through the ocean, big enough that it went smoothly over the waves, but small enough that Tuck didn't feel like he was trying to show off by chartering it for just the two of them. The captain was an older gentleman who was doing a good job of giving them their space.

Tuck watched Maryn as she leaned back and closed her eyes. The sun was on her face and the wind pushed her hair back. A simple pink sundress showed off her tan shoulders and slender neck. She was gorgeous. He couldn't believe he'd wasted two weeks before coming to see her, but the fact still remained that she left. He wanted to talk to her about it, but didn't want to interrupt the lighthearted mood that had been with them from the minute he picked her up this morning and asked her to grab a swimsuit.

"Yes!" she'd exclaimed and given him a quick hug before dashing back into her bedroom.

Tuck wished he could've kept her in his arms, kissed her like he did yesterday. Her flowery smell seemed to linger even after she pulled away. Yet, he knew he had to take things slow and not scare her off. Being with her again was everything he'd hoped. He felt complete and alive and happier than he'd been in his entire life when she was around.

She opened her eyes and grinned at him. "You are staring at me, sir."

"You're worth staring at, ma'am." He winked.

She licked her lips and leaned forward. "So are you. Has anyone told you that you look like Superman, not the old one, the new one, I can't remember the actor's name but when he like comes out of the water after he saves those people on the oil rig and you think maybe he drowned and he's all buff and hairy, but I guess he has blue eyes where yours are dark and your hair is longer... what?"

He wanted to tell her how much he'd missed her, listening to her talk, the way she made him feel like Superman. He definitely wasn't that shredded so he wasn't sure about her analogy. "Superman, huh?"

She grinned. "My own personal Superman."

The boat captain looked back at them and smiled. Tucker returned the smile, but couldn't keep his eyes off Maryn.

"So, you've kidnapped me on this beautiful boat and now we're going to just jet around the ocean all day?"

"You should know me better than that." Even as he said it he realized she didn't know him very well. They just hadn't had enough time together.

"Yes." She nodded. "All that pent-up energy. Sitting for more than an hour probably kills you. How do you do your programming?"

"Adjustable desk."

She smiled. "Lucky. So... what do you have planned for my playing hooky from work pleasure today?"

"You're just going to have to wait and see."

She leaned back, closed her eyes again, and muttered, "I don't like waiting."

Tucker laughed. She claimed he had pent-up energy, she was like the Energizer Bunny and he loved every minute he spent with her.

They pulled into a dock on Catalina Island a few minutes later. Tuck tipped the captain and told him he'd text when they were ready to leave. The man brushed his fingers along his cap. "Best of luck with your day."

"Thanks." Tucker thought that he didn't need luck, he already had Maryn by his side and that was all he needed.

He reached for her hand as they walked off the dock and she fit her small hand in his larger one. Tuck grinned. The island breeze, a day of no work and all Maryn.

Directing her toward Catalina Island Golf Cart Rental, he told them his name and within a few minutes they were seated in a golf cart.

"I love that you rented a golf cart."

Tucker shrugged. "It's the best way to see this island."

"Yeah, but how many billionaires do you know who drive a p. o. s. golf cart instead of proving how rich they are by renting a helicopter or something."

"I'm the only billionaire I know, so I'd say a hundred percent. Did you want a helicopter?"

"Oh, no way. I'd much rather see the island like this." She gave him a little side hug and Tucker's breath caught. She was acting more comfortable around him by the minute, maybe by the end of the day he'd be able to kiss her again. A guy could hope.

Out of the corner of his eye, he saw a man watching them from the side of the rental shop. He was average-sized with deeply-tanned skin, a bright Hawaiian print shirt, and pants riding so low Tucker wasn't sure how he kept them on. When he saw Tucker watching him, he turned and disappeared behind the building.

Tucker knew the guy was probably harmless. Maryn turned a lot of heads and he understood if the guy was checking her out, but it still bothered him. Pressing the gas down, he was surprised when the golf cart shot forward. "Underestimated the power of this beauty."

Maryn's tinkling laughter and her hand grabbing his as he turned a corner too fast made him push the guy to the back of his mind. He'd ride a p. o. s. golf cart every day if he could have this. They cruised around the island, taking their time as he showed her Chimes Tower, Avalon Harbor, and the Zane Grey Hotel. She said she'd grown up poor, but he was still surprised she'd never been here.

"Zane Grey, the author?"

"Yeah. Too bad it's closed. It's a cool location to stay."

Maryn leaned back slightly and Tucker wondered what he'd said wrong.

They took their time driving around some rutted back streets through the trees and then made their way back into town. Tucker pulled into the entry of the Edgewater Hotel. Maryn climbed out of the golf cart and eyed him strangely. He gave the valet money to return the golf cart to the rental place, got the key from the front desk, and escorted her to the elevator. He could've sworn that same guy with the Hawaiian shirt was in the lobby, but when he searched for him, he had disappeared. He was being far too paranoid, but he felt a fierce protection toward Maryn and didn't want some schmuck checking her out.

Maryn folded her arms across her middle and didn't talk or meet his gaze in the elevator. Oh, no. What had he done wrong? She was being much too quiet. When he unlocked the door to the suite she marched inside, tossed her bag on the couch, and folded her arms across her chest. "You didn't tell me it was an *overnight* date. I would've packed differently." Her voice was cold and distant.

Tuck's breath whooshed out of him. He held up both hands. "Oh, no, Maryn. Oh. The room. You thought..."

"What did you expect me to think?" She arched her eyebrows and glared at him.

"But you know I wouldn't try to..." He shook his head.

"I've spent three days with you, Tuck. How am I supposed to know you so well? You don't know me that well either. I thought maybe you would assume I might want this after I let you sleep in the bed with me in Island Park."

She gnawed at her lip and Tucker had to force himself to not get distracted at the mention of snuggling through the night and the way her teeth tugged at those soft lips.

"No. I didn't think that. I apologize, Maryn. I got the room so we'd have a place to change now and shower after we play in the water. I also wanted to have access to this beach. It's a nice quiet one. Plus I love Maggie's Blue Rose for lunch and Lloyd's for candy and there are two bedrooms and two bathrooms so I promise you will have lots of privacy. All the privacy you want." Tucker stopped at the amused look on Maryn's face. "You make me talk more than I ever have in my life."

"Especially when you're in trouble." She tilted her head to the side.

"Please forgive me."

Maryn smiled and he let himself breathe again. "You're forgiven. I'm sorry for assuming."

"You had every right to. Lunch first or beach?"

"Lunch on the beach sounds good."

"Yes, it does. I'll call in some food then go change in my *private* bedroom."

She smirked and he knew she'd forgiven him. He cursed

himself for being so stupid and not explaining when they pulled up to the hotel. His dating experience was much too limited.

Maryn liked the quiet little beach. The front desk handed Tucker two beach chairs, an umbrella, and a small cooler with treats and drinks. Maryn carried a platter of shrimp, lobster, and chicken tacos from Maggie's Blue Rose. She felt so stupid for assuming that Tucker wanted to spend the night with her. He'd proven himself a gentleman in Island Park and just because of James' stupid insinuations she'd gotten all bratty and judgmental. Again, Tucker had shown his true character when he didn't get upset, but apologized to her instead. Maybe he was too good to be true, but she was going to enjoy each moment they had together.

She took off her cover up and relaxed into the chair. She sighed as Tuck took his shirt off and didn't hide that she was ogling him. He was broad and had lots of evident muscles, but Maryn loved that he didn't have some chiseled abdomen, just a normal one. It was obvious he worked hard, but he didn't spend his life in the gym trying to form the perfect body. Tucker Shaffer had more purpose than that and she loved it.

"You're um, staring," he said, folding his arms across his chest and making her stare more at the breadth of those biceps.

"So are you," she shot back.

"Yeah, but you're perfect and worth staring at."

"So are you."

He grimaced. "I'm not sure about that."

"I love your shape," she said then she rotated around and tugged down the back of her one-piece swimsuit to show him her scars. The skin had healed, but it was still pink and bumpy. "I'm definitely not perfect."

Tuck groaned, sank down on the chair next to her, and traced his fingers over the scars on her lower back. Maryn trembled from the soft touch of his calloused fingers. "It kills me that I did this to you."

Maryn flipped back around to face him. "You didn't do it. That grumpy ten-foot tall bear is to blame."

Tuck smiled. "I still feel responsible."

"Well, don't. It's going to be fine. The scars will fade soon and all we'll have is the memories." The image of him standing between her and the bear would never go away, but she hoped they'd have more together than the memories. She reclined into her chair and chose one of the shrimp tacos from the platter. They ate in silence for a few minutes, the laughter of children, the gentle lapping of the ocean against the sand in the bay, and the squawking of sea gulls their entertainment. Maryn ate a lobster taco next then had to drink some strawberry lemonade to cut the spice.

"So," Maryn said, "we're just going to chill on the beach all day."

"You know me better than that."

Maryn giggled. "What's next?"

"Come for a walk with me." He stood and offered his hand. Maryn had no problem placing her hand in his. They walked slowly down the beach.

"How are Mama Porter, Johnson, and Braxton?" she asked.

"Good. They all miss you."

"Ah. I miss them too, you were all so good to me." She hoped he knew she meant him as much as anyone. "They're in Island Park until Christmas?"

"No. We all came to the Laguna Beach house."

"What?" She stopped walking and turned to face him. "You stay in Island Park until Christmas and then you go to Grand Cayman. I know, you told me. This is pertinent information, why didn't you share it the moment you saw me?"

Tuck slipped a strand of hair behind her ear and glanced so tenderly at her it was all she could do to not throw herself at him. "I didn't know how to tell you that we changed our plans because I wanted to be closer to you."

Maryn stepped back, plunged into the moat of a sand castle, and would've fallen if Tuck hadn't reached out and steadied her. He didn't release her arm and Maryn decided to change directions and take a step closer to him. She placed her hands on his broad chest, the smooth skin feeling much too nice, and tilted her head to the side. "So, you want more publicity from *The Rising Star*, huh?"

Chuckling, he shook his head. "Please, no. Though I did enjoy the article. Thank you for painting me in such a good light."

"It wasn't hard to do. You're an impressive man, Tucker Shaffer." She trailed her hands along his chest and up to his muscular shoulders. He quivered a bit and she liked knowing her touch affected him.

"Impressive enough that today won't be our last date?"

"I don't know." She bit at her lip. "Depends on how good you can kiss."

"Oh, I can kiss." He framed her face with his hands, lowered his head to hers, and explored her mouth with a tender passion that had her tingling.

"Yes, you can," Maryn whispered and kissed him again, happiness and desire coursing through her.

They broke apart a few minutes later and Tucker walked her to a spot that rented paddle boards, snorkeling equipment, and offered parasailing tours.

"So, what do you want to do first?"

Maryn grinned. "All of it!"

Tucker smiled. "Can we parasail together?" he asked the surf bum-looking guy who was helping them.

"Best way to do it." The guy winked at her.

Maryn squeezed Tucker's hand, but hoped he didn't feel her tremble slightly. She'd wanted to parasail since she was a little girl, but she was terrified of heights. "This is going to rock!"

He laughed.

A few minutes later they were on the boat headed out into the bay, all strapped into parasailing equipment. Maryn's stomach tumbled. She wanted to do this. She wanted to do it with Tucker, but what if the umbrella ripped and they tumbled to their deaths or she went insane and launched herself into the air? She always had the craziest thoughts when she was up high.

Tuck squeezed her hand and leaned close. "You okay?"

"Sure, sure, why do you ask?"

"You're hands are shaking and your face is pale."

"You two ready?" the guy asked, checking their equipment one more time as the boat cut its engine and floated.

"Yes!" Maryn said.

"You sure?" Tucker asked.

She nodded to him. "Just let me pray." Closing her eyes, she prayed for strength and protection. She opened her eyes to Tucker staring at her. "I'm good. I promise."

The dude lifted the sail into the air and it caught the wind. At the same time the boat driver eased the engine into gear and they glided forward. Maryn and Tucker jerked when the rope attached to the parasail ran out of slack and then rose slowly up. Tucker reached over and wrapped his hand around hers. Maryn gripped his hand like a lifeline.

"I guess this isn't the best time to tell you this," she managed to squeak out, "but I'm terrified of heights."

They were going higher and higher. The boat driver gunned it and instead of floating they started flying through the air. Maryn screamed.

"Do you want to stop?" Tucker asked.

"No way! This is awesome! Yahoo!" Maryn hollered. Her hair blew behind them in the wind. She closed her eyes to savor the touch of the sun and the breeze.

Tucker laughed.

The boat slowed and they floated down and almost dipped in the water before the driver gunned the engine and they shot forward then up again. Maryn giggled from the butterflies in her stomach. This was much better than a rollercoaster ride. She wasn't ready to puke and she was actually enjoying the sensation. Her mom had never been able to afford theme parks but Alyssa's dad had taken them to Disneyland a few times and she absolutely hated the drops in height on the rides. But this was different, and much more enjoyable.

She realized she was clinging to Tucker's hand. She let go. "Sorry. I really am loving it."

"You promise?"

"Yes."

They were floating along now and the view of the boats, beach, and island vegetation was beautiful.

"You don't ever have to do anything you don't want to do when you're with me," Tuck said.

She turned her gaze from the view to his deep brown eyes. "I know that, Tuck." She paused and flung out a hand to encompass the beautiful ocean. "I've wanted to do this for so long, but never been brave enough. Thank you."

He grinned. "I'd like to make more of your dreams come true."

Maryn's breath caught at the implication. The boat slowed at the same time and they dipped down. She cried out in surprise then laughed. When they levelled out again, she said, "I'm holding you to that."

Chapter Sixteen

They were turning in their snorkeling gear after a decent snorkel at Lover's Cove when Tucker felt eyes on him. He spun around and Hawaiian shirt was staring at him. The guy ducked into the bathroom.

"Excuse me for a minute," he said to Maryn. Her hair was plastered to her head from the snorkeling gear and water. Her bright blue eyes sparkled at him and he couldn't help but smile at her.

"Sure. I'll just wait down on the beach."

"I'll get your paddle boards down there and waiting for you," Travis, the bleached-blond guy who'd helped them all day, said.

"Thank you." Tucker gave Maryn one more smile before striding to the bathroom. Banging into the bathroom, he looked around, but it appeared to be empty. He used the urinal, flushed, washed his hands, and then pushed open the door. Letting the door close again, he didn't move. Five seconds later, Hawaiian shirt came out of a stall.

The guy swore loudly when he saw him. Tuck walked slowly to him and didn't touch him, but he got in his space. "Why are you following us?"

"I-I'm not." The guy's black eyes darted around the bathroom, anywhere but at Tuck.

"Do I look like somebody you want to mess with?"

The guy finally met his eye and shook his head quickly. He backed toward the wall.

"Be square with me and I might not rough you up." Tuck didn't like to threaten, but he wanted some answers. He probably could've offered the guy money and got faster results, but he hated bribes worse than threats and he was ticked that this guy was following them.

"I'm not watching you," the guy's voice quavered. "Please. Just let me go."

Tucker took a step closer. "Tell me now!"

"I'm watching the girl."

"Why?" That was what he feared.

"She's hot." A quick grin flitted across his face but left quickly.

Tucker grabbed his shirt and slammed him into the wall. "So you want to get beat?"

"No! Sorry." The guy was shaking now and Tucker would've felt bad for him if he wasn't so angry. "I got paid to follow her. That's all. The guy just wanted to make sure she was okay."

That was a punch in the gut. Somebody was afraid Tucker would mistreat Maryn? "Who paid you?"

"I don't have a name. Preppy dude. Dressed real nice. Blond hair."

"How long have you been following her?"

"Just for today." The guy squirmed, but didn't try to push his way to freedom.

"From her apartment?" Tucker wondered if it was that James guy. It would actually make him feel better if it was, a jealous ex-boyfriend was better than a stalker or worse.

"Yeah, he gave me the address and told me to be there before eight, follow you two wherever you went, and make sure she was safe. I caught the ferry over and found you."

The Feisty One

Tucker bent down a few inches, his fingers curled around the guy's shirt until he heard the fabric rip. He waited a couple more seconds before speaking, "Tell whoever paid you to back off. Maryn is mine and no one is messing with her." His face flushed as he said it. He had no rights to Maryn and maybe the guy who sent this dude really wasn't looking to hurt her, but he wanted the message sent anyway, just in case. "Got it?"

"Sure, man."

Tucker released him. "How'd he find you?"

The guy straightened his shirt and studied the sink behind Tucker. "I work for an agency that does private investigating and this sort of stuff."

"What were you going to do if I did hurt her?"

The guy's gaze flitted over him then quickly away. "When I saw how big you were I had to change my game plan. I would've called the cops."

Tucker nodded, grateful this guy seemed to be on the up. "Good plan." He turned and banged out the bathroom door. Luckily, it was a decent walk to the beach. He needed that few minutes to calm down. It was bothersome and scary that someone was tracking Maryn. Should he tell her?

When he saw Maryn in her bright pink and blue swirled swimsuit, trying to balance on a paddle board, all those protective instincts fired again. He wanted to be the one to take care of her and make sure no one hurt her. What right did that guy have to pay someone to follow her?

He watched her for a minute, enjoying the way she looked in her suit that was fitted but modest. Her shape was definitely beautiful and she could've looked amazing in a string bikini, but he liked that she didn't feel the need to display everything.

Maryn lost her balance and with a little scream fell into the water. It was only a foot deep so she didn't go all the way under. Tucker couldn't help but laugh. She saw him and called out, "Come on! You need to share in some humiliation. This isn't easy on waves."

Tucker jogged to the water's edge then plunged through to her side. He lifted her onto the board and kept his hands at her waist steadying her. Touching her never failed to get his blood pumping. "You just need me teaching you."

"Maybe I just need you." Maryn winked and Tucker's chest swelled. He hoped she really did.

Their day together had been near perfect, but Maryn didn't want it to end. As they got into his Lexus parked next to the Dana Point Harbor, Maryn asked, "Can we go see Mama Porter, Johnson, and Braxton?"

"They'd love that. You know Mama Porter will make you stay for dinner."

She fingered her hair. She'd showered before they left the island, but without any product, her blonde locks were looking pretty frizzy. Tuck didn't seem to be bothered by her make-up free appearance. "No way would I miss out on Mama Porter's cooking." Though it was more about staying with Tucker longer.

"Let me text them to make sure Johnson is home. He's been busy lately with some real estate transactions but he'd be mad if he missed you."

The drive was only about fifteen minutes. Tuck parked out front and got Maryn's door. The house was impressive, not that

142

she'd expected anything different. It was three sprawling stories, overlooking Laguna Beach. She had a hard time appreciating the arches and columns or the stucco entrance as Braxton swung the door open. She ran to him and gave him a hug. He was stiff but smiling. "Ms. Howe. It's wonderful to see you again."

"You too, Mr. Braxton."

"Did you recover well?"

"Perfectly. You're the best stitcher upper a girl could ask for."

His starched exterior seemed to be cracking as he almost grinned at her.

"Would you look who's here?" Johnson called from a formal room off to the right. He swept her into a bear hug. "Glad the big guy finally grew a brain," he muttered.

"I heard that," Tucker said.

"I don't care." Johnson winked at her.

"My girl!" Mama Porter shrieked and ran to her. She squeezed Maryn into her generous bosom and wouldn't let go. "We've been so worried. Are you okay? We all missed you so much." She finally let go and darted a glance at Tucker.

Maryn looked at Tucker as well. He smiled at them, his dark eyes glinting with delicious promise. She wanted to run her fingers through his hair and be alone with him until she got tired of him. No, she'd have a hard time getting tired of him.

"Well." Mama Porter interrupted their glancing communication. "I'll just go check on dinner while Tucker gives you a tour. You are staying for dinner?"

"I wouldn't miss your cooking," Maryn reassured her.

"Perfect."

"Thank you."

"No, thank you," Johnson said. "She hasn't cooked this much

143

good food in weeks." He winked at her then he and Braxton followed Mama Porter.

Maryn turned to Tucker. "It's so good to see them all."

"We all really missed you."

Maryn held his gaze. "All of you?"

"Some of us more than others."

She flushed with pleasure, too happy to respond to that. Tucker placed his hand on her lower back and escorted her through the formal rooms on the main floor and then onto a huge deck that overlooked a lush flower garden, trees, and the ocean beyond. The house was on a cliff, but had a staircase down to the beach. Maryn could definitely get used to living in a place like this. She stared at the view, inhaling the scent of plumeria and imagined running on the beach every morning and sitting on the huge patio overlooking the ocean at night. Most of all, she imagined it with Tucker by her side. She needed to slow down her imagination.

"It's beautiful here," she said. "I love the feeling in your houses."

Tucker rested a hand on the window frame above her head, his body inches away from her side. "Even when you ran away in Island Park?"

Maryn turned to face him. He was so close she had to arch her head back to meet his gaze and she barely resisted wrapping her arms around his waist. "That was a stupid misunderstanding."

Tucker studied her. "Forgive me for being scary?"

"Yes," Maryn whispered. "But remember what we talked about, have you forgiven yourself?"

"For hurting you?" He traced his finger along her chin and across her lips. "That's a tough one."

Maryn trembled from his touch, but knew she had to talk to

him about this. "I'm talking about the things you had to do in the Army."

He didn't move, but his body stiffened. "Since you left... I've tried to pray."

"You have?"

"It's definitely a struggle to put it behind me, but I have felt some peace."

Maryn smiled up at him. "The forgiveness will come. You're a good man, Tucker Shaffer."

"Thanks." He swallowed. "I wanted to know that you could forgive me. I've blamed myself for you getting hurt."

"No." She shook her head. "I forgave you the instant you turned into Superman and saved my life."

He smirked at the Superman reference, rested his other hand next to her head, effectively framing her face, and scooted closer. His large body brushed against hers and Maryn caught a breath, her heart beating a staccato so sharp she wondered if he could feel it.

"I'm good at forgiving," she told him, unable to keep her gaze from straying to his lips before going back to those chocolate fudge eyes that seemed to see into her. He was serious about life, but still made her feel light and happy. "I forgive everyone, kind of like an eel, it all just slides right off my slippery back."

Tucker grinned and lowered his head closer to hers. "Good way to be."

She giggled as his breath touched her lips. He smelled like that wonderful mixture of lime, jasmine, and salt water that was uniquely Tuck. Had he brought a bottle of cologne with him to Catalina? He'd had a small bag. She'd been so excited this morning she hadn't thought to pack much more than her suit and probably smelled like rotten fish.

"Yep, Granny Ellie was always telling us to love our enemies, it would drive them crazy." Her mouth kept running even though she wasn't concentrating on what she was saying, just hoping he would kiss her. "Not that you were my enemy, you could never be my enemy. Even though I was scared of you for a minute, I know that wasn't the real you. I like you, the real you, very much. You're very heroic and I don't think I could ever be afraid when you're with me." She paused for a breath, but had a hard time catching one with the way he was grinning at her.

"Maryn?" His deep voice rumbled through her chest, they were that close.

"Yes?" She bit at her lip and prayed she could stop talking long enough to kiss him.

"Do you think you could stop talking for a minute while I kissed you?"

Maryn laughed. Her eyes flickered from his amused gaze down to those lips again. His lips were soft, commanding, and such a great shape—the top lip had a slight bow and the bottom lip was just full enough to make things interesting. She'd daydreamed about those lips and about the little scar next to them. "Maybe one minute."

He smiled and pressed his lips to hers. Maryn sighed from the pleasure and contentment that shot through her. "Or two," she whispered, running her hands up his chest to entangle them in his hair.

Tuck placed one hand on her cheek and slid the other one down her waist, bringing her even closer to him. He took advantage of her lips for several wonderful seconds. Maryn arched up on her toes, molding her body to his, returning kiss for kiss.

He groaned and kissed her jawline. "Or maybe twenty," Maryn murmured.

Tuck chuckled and then captured her lips again. He lifted her completely off her feet, kissing her more thoroughly then she'd ever been kissed.

A door opened and closed and then feet tapping a staccato on the wood deck and a soft, "Ahem," should've pulled them apart, but they were in their own world.

Finally, Tucker set her down, but didn't let her out of the circle of his arms. "Yes, Brax?" he growled. His face pressed against Maryn's.

"Mama Porter has informed me that dinner is ready."

"Thanks, Brax," Tuck said, running his hand through Maryn's hair and not looking at his friend.

"Very good. We'll see you in a minute?" It sounded like Braxton was having a hard time not laughing.

"Or two," Tuck responded, winking at Maryn and gently rubbing his nose against hers.

Braxton harrumphed and marched away.

"Or twenty," Maryn said, pulling his head down again.

Tucker kissed her with a grin on his face. Maryn knew she should feel bad that Mama Porter's delicious food was getting cold, but with Tucker kissing her like this, she didn't have an appetite for anything else.

Chapter Seventeen

The next night Maryn knew she had to go with James and sort out their friendship, but she wished every day could be like yesterday—spent in its entirety with Tucker Shaffer and lots of kissing at the end.

After a delicious dinner with very few awkward pauses and bantering like they used to do before all this drama came into their relationship, James tugged Maryn out of her seat on the rooftop of Perch, a French bistro that Maryn enjoyed but thought was overpriced. The view of the city was amazing up here and it was a beautiful, mild night.

Now if she could get brave enough to tell James she was dating Tucker exclusively. Not that Tucker had asked that of her, but she wanted to do it. Committing herself to more with Tucker was exactly what she wanted in her life.

She smiled just thinking of Tuck. Their day yesterday kept playing through her mind, especially those kisses on his patio last night. Oh, my, he was the whole package for her—fun, kind, thoughtful, handsome, kissed like a rock star.

The wind whipped her hair and she pulled it away from her face. James escorted her toward the glass wall, his hand a bit more possessive than she would've liked through the thin material of her blue sheath cocktail dress.

They gazed out over the city lights and didn't say anything for a few minutes.

"Thanks for coming with me tonight," James said.

"Sure. It's been fun to catch up, kind of like old times." She swallowed hard and forced a smile. "James I need to tell you—"

He put his fingers on her lips and cut her off. Maryn leaned away from the awkward pushing of his first and second fingers.

"Please. I need to say this first." He looked out at the city then focused on her. "I know I've asked you to marry me a dozen times and you always tease me and somehow say no without breaking my heart."

Oh, crap. Oh, no. This was *not* a good start to the breakup talk. "James..."

"Mar... I love you." His blue eyes sparkled. "We just fit together, you and I. I love working with you, being with you. You're beautiful, smart, fun. I can spend my whole life just listening to your funny expressions and laughing with you. Please say you'll marry me." He pulled a ring box out of his suit coat and popped it open.

For the first time in Maryn's life, she was temporarily speechless. If James' sweet words hadn't knocked out her communication skills, this ring would certainly do it. The center diamond had to be over three karats with dozens of smaller diamonds embedded in the white gold and building up to surround the main diamond. It was obviously expensive, gaudy, and not her style at all. She truly hated it.

She looked into James' expectant face. They had been close friends for years, but she didn't love him, had never loved him like that. Even if she hadn't fallen for Tucker, she knew she would never be able to marry James.

"James. I'm so grateful for your friendship and really appreciate that beautiful speech, but I'm sorry." His smile drooped. She tried again, "You and I are not really..." She glanced at the diamond ring then back up at him. "How in the criminy did you afford this monstrosity?"

James' face paled then mottled red spots appeared in his cheeks. He snapped the box shut and jammed it into his suit pocket. "I guess that's Maryn's twisted way of saying no."

Maryn shook her head and backed away. "I know what your take home is, and it's not much more than I make. What are you *doing*, James?" Maryn's breath caught at the furious look on his face.

"So now I can't afford a ring for the woman I love?" He quickly glanced around, but nobody was paying them any attention. He grabbed her arm and his fingers dug into her flesh. "So I'm not the billionaire *Tucker Shaffer*." He spit out the name that Maryn drooled over. "And suddenly I'm not good enough for you. I can provide anything he can, Maryn, you have to trust me on this. I'm doing this for you."

She yanked her arm free. "It's not about money, James. It's about my best friend changing and buying things he shouldn't be able to afford. This isn't like you. Please, talk to me. I can help you with whatever you've gotten into. Is it drugs? Embezzling?"

He laughed harshly. "You have no idea what you're talking about. If you dare try to insinuate anything, I will ruin your career faster than you can imagine. Good luck with your beastly hermit." He turned on his heel and marched to the elevator.

Maryn didn't move. James was doing something illegal. She knew it. The threat to her career would've frozen her even a few weeks ago, but knowing Tuck had altered the way she looked at her life. Even though Tuck was insanely wealthy, he didn't care about climbing career ladders or impressing people. He spent his time helping others and doing something meaningful.

The waiter set a bill on their table and glanced around until he met Maryn's eye. He was probably realizing he was about to get stiffed. Maryn sighed, walked back to the table, and pulled out her credit card.

The night dragged for Tucker. He tried to work, but couldn't get anything productive done. Mama Tucker and Braxton had gone out to dinner and who knew where Johnson was. He wished at least Johnson was around to... do something with.

The thought of Maryn with that preppy idiot had him pacing the floor and saying quick prayers that Maryn wouldn't fall into James' traps and that if James tried to kiss her she would push him away. He wondered briefly if the Lord thought his prayers were odd or out of line, but he kept offering them anyway.

Finally, he sat on his back patio and just listened to the waves crash. He dropped his head back against the soft cushion of the patio chair and sighed. He had everything that most people thought they wanted in their lives—too much money, good health, trustworthy friends—but he was reduced to a worrywart over this beautiful blonde that he couldn't get enough of.

He pulled his phone out and studied it. Eleven p.m. Was it too late to call her, too early? What if he interrupted something with James? That thought had him pushing her number on the recent call list as fast as he could.

Maryn wrapped up in a blanket and shivered on the couch. What could she do to help James? She had no proof he was doing something illegal, but he'd changed since she'd come back from

151

Island Park and she didn't think it was just because of his jealousy over Tucker.

Her phone rang. She saw his picture and sighed, "Tuck."

"Hey. How'd your night go?"

"Miserable. I told him I wouldn't marry him and he stuck me with the bill."

"Ouch. Wish I could've been there."

"Why?" She laughed and stood to pace her small apartment.

"I'd still like to pummel him for you."

"Be my guest." She felt guilty as she said it. James was obviously in some trouble and she didn't want any harm to come to her friend. She pushed thoughts of James away. "So, I was going to call you."

"Yeah?"

Maryn was surprised that she felt nervous. This was Tucker. Sure, she didn't know everything about him, but she did know he wanted to be with her. At least he'd given her every indication of that. "Can I take you out tomorrow night?"

"You're not taking me out."

Ouch. She grabbed onto the back of the couch and swallowed hard. "Why not?"

"Because I get to take you out. I'm the man."

Maryn sighed in relief and did a little shimmy, rubbing her palms together. He wanted to go out with her. "Chauvinist."

"Whatever happened to the word gentleman?"

"Yes, you definitely are that too."

He chuckled.

Maryn pressed the phone closer to her ear. "I love your laugh."

"Oh?"

"I could listen to it all night." She walked into her room and lay down.

"I love your laugh too, it's like this tinkling bell." His voice lowered. "And I love a lot more about you than your laugh."

"Oh?"

"The list is very, very long."

Maryn smiled and stretched out on her bed. "Maybe you can tell me all about that list on our date tomorrow night." *After you kiss me senseless.* She almost giggled at her girlish longings.

"Which *I* am taking *you* on."

She shook her head. "We'll see about that. If you haven't noticed I'm a bit opinionated and usually get my way."

"I hadn't noticed."

She smiled. "My friends, Alyssa and Beck, are back from whatever corner of the world they were saving and they want to meet you."

"Should I be nervous?"

"Definitely. If they don't give their stamp of approval," she made a clinching sound with her teeth, "you're out."

"Ooh. This is serious. I'll be on my best behavior."

"You'd better be. I'll pick you up at 6:30. Dress nice."

"No, I'll pick *you* up at 6:30." His voice lowered. "You can wear whatever you want to."

She tried for an irritated sigh but it came out like a lovesick moan.

"Maybe you could wear my shirt," he said. "That looked great on you."

"I wear it to bed almost every night."

"Oh?" His voice was husky and driving her crazy, in the best way possible. "I like that."

"I know you do." She paused and forced herself to change the subject. "Do you even want to know where we're going?"

153

"I'll be with you. The rest is just details."

She did sigh then. "See you tomorrow."

"Wish it was already here."

"Bye," she whispered.

"Bye," his voice was deep, throaty, and absolutely inspiring. If it wasn't past midnight and Mama Porter or Braxton wouldn't catch them, she'd be driving across town right now. "You have to hang up first," he said.

Maryn laughed. "I feel like I'm back in junior high."

"I didn't have any gorgeous blondes asking me out in junior high."

"They didn't know what they were missing."

He chuckled.

Maryn smiled. "Okay, I'm hanging up now."

"Thanks. I couldn't bring myself to do it first."

"See you tomorrow." She hit the end call button quickly like ripping off a Band-Aid then held the phone to her chest. Ah, Tucker Shaffer. She'd have sweet dreams tonight.

Chapter Eighteen

Maryn loved the way Tucker looked in a gray button down shirt left untucked over jeans and a navy blazer. His kind smile was the perfect contrast to his strong face and body and the flowing hair. She was smitten. He escorted her with an arm around her waist into the Beachfront Restaurant in the Jamaican Bay Inn. Maryn wore a red knee-length lace dress with strappy black and white checked heels. She leaned into Tucker.

Alyssa and Beck were already at the table. Maryn introduced Tuck and watched carefully as he shook her friends' hands and exchanged greetings. He was bigger than Beck. She never thought she'd fall for a guy who was bigger than Beck as Beck had always seemed like this huge dude, but Tucker felt right to her.

"You've been in Honduras doing humanitarian work?" Tucker asked after the waiter took their drink orders and left them to peruse the menu.

"Have you heard of Jordan's Buds?" Beck asked, his blue eyes focused on Tucker.

"Yes." He smiled at Maryn. "Maryn's been telling me about it, but I actually worked in an orphanage outside of Belize that you donate to. The Liberty Children's Home. I remember reading about Jordan's Buds on some plaques they have."

"Oh, yeah? The director there is great, but it's hard to see so many HIV positive children."

Tuck nodded his agreement. "Do you always work with children?"

"Yes. The foundation is named after my brother. He was only eight when he died, so it fit."

Maryn had never heard Beck talk about his brother. Alyssa caught her eye and lifted one shoulder.

"I'm sorry about your brother," Tuck said.

"Thank you." He cleared his throat and changed the subject. "Maryn has been bragging you up like you're a superhero. It's great to finally be able to get to know you a little bit."

Tuck laughed and squeezed her hand. "I was excited to meet both of you as well. Especially the amazing A.A. I have some of your photos."

"Thanks, but I want to hear about this bear attack." Alyssa's dark eyes sparkled. "I've heard Maryn's rendition, but she was so dreamy about you she could barely tell me what happened."

Maryn stuck her tongue out at Alyssa. Leave it to her best friend to make her look like a sappy sucker.

Alyssa glanced up at Beck, all twitterpated. They were a beautiful couple with their dark coloring. "It reminded me of when Beck saved me from a druggie on Maui."

Beck grinned at her and stole a quick kiss.

"I'd rather hear that story," Tucker said.

"Nope." Alyssa shook her head. "We're hearing about your heroics first."

Tucker's face reddened. He turned to Maryn and placed his arm around the back of her chair. "Maryn's trying to make me into some hero, but she shouldn't have even been out in that storm."

Maryn arched an eyebrow at him and squeezed his knee. He jumped slightly. "That is not your fault and I have every right to call you a hero."

He smiled down at her. They were lost in their own world when the waiter appeared and took their dinner order. Maryn told him she'd have the special, without any clue what the special was.

The night progressed and Tucker seemed to be at ease and enjoying himself with her friends. When Tuck and Beck were discussing hockey at great lengths, Alyssa leaned over and whispered, "Good job, sis. I like him and it's obvious Beck approves."

"He's so great," she said, "his hotness is just a bonus."

"*Almost* as hot as Beck."

Maryn laughed. "He's smoking past Beck."

"Not possible." Alyssa giggled, but then quieted as they noticed the men had paused their conversation and were studying the two of them. "Sorry," Alyssa said. "Girl talk."

The waiter brought their food and Alyssa was asking him for some kind of sauce. Tucker bent next to her ear and whispered, "I'm smoking hot?"

Maryn bit at her lip. "You know it."

He chuckled, thanked the waiter, and proceeded to cut into his steak. Maryn took a bite of her mahi-mahi, savoring the fresh burst of flavor. Beck started teasing her about being another one of the friends to fulfill the Billionaire Bride Pact. She blushed furiously and told him, "In Tuck's dreams."

Tuck nodded. "She's right."

The blush deepened along with happy bubbles filling her stomach. She knew she and Tuck were a long ways from a proposal, but thankfully he hadn't gotten awkward with Beck's teasing, just taken it in stride.

She ate the asparagus and risotto, saving the rest of the mahi mahi for the end. Enjoying the last few bites, she could envision many more dinners with the four of them. Her eyes pricked as she realized that because of Tuck she was no longer lonely.

The restaurant suddenly seemed to buzz with conversation and loud footsteps and then it got horribly quiet. Maryn spun in her chair to see four policemen stride toward them and then surround their intimate table. Tuck and Beck both sprung to their feet and stepped in front of Maryn and Alyssa.

"Tucker Shaffer?" a short policeman with a full head of curly red hair asked.

"Yes, sir."

"You're under arrest for the murder of Jaron Underwood."

Tucker's brow furrowed. "Excuse me?"

The officer started reciting Tucker's rights while Maryn thought she was going to black out. She stood and clung to Tucker's arm. "What is happening?"

"I have no idea," he muttered. He squeezed her hand and mustered a smile. "It's got to be a mistake. We'll get it figured out."

Beck and Alyssa looked to be in shock. Neither of them moved for a few seconds. People at surrounding tables were gaping at the scene. A few cameras flashed from phones. Maryn's heart pounded in her head. She held onto Tucker's hand, hoping he would stay calm and not sure if she could let him go with the police. Arrested for murder? This wasn't happening.

"Now, wait a minute," Beck said. "This is obviously a mistake. You can't just arrest him."

"Watch me," the police officer said, pulling out a set of handcuffs. The other officers closed ranks.

Tucker lifted his hands. "I'll go. It'll be fine." He nodded to Beck. "I'm sure it's a mistake and we'll figure it out quick." His voice lowered. "Please don't handcuff me here." He gestured to Maryn and the officer nodded then grasped his elbow.

"I'm sorry," Tucker said to Alyssa and Beck.

"You shouldn't be apologizing," Beck said. "Do you have a legal team to figure this out?"

Tucker nodded. He looked to Maryn. "I didn't murder anyone. You believe me?"

"Yes," she said, glaring at the police.

He moved to pull his wallet out of his back pocket. The policeman all tensed. Two pulled their weapons.

Maryn gasped.

"I just want to leave money for dinner," Tucker explained. The redhead guy nodded. Tuck threw a couple of hundred dollar bills down.

Beck shook his head to protest, but they were already leading Tucker away. Maryn watched him go, tears pooling at the corner of her eyes. For some reason she remembered last night when James had stuck her with the bill because he was angry with her. Tucker was being arrested and he was thoughtful enough to cover everyone's dinner. She sighed, but then her insides clenched. Murder? Really? Tuck had to be innocent, he just had to be. But there was a small part of her that knew he had a temper and knew how to use a weapon. No. She couldn't think like that. She had to do everything in her power to prove his innocence.

Her legs wobbled and she held onto the chair and sank heavily into it. Beck was on his phone, gesturing angrily. Alyssa knelt in front of her. "Are you okay, sweetie?"

Maryn was horribly cold and so alone without Tuck. "No, not really."

"Let's get out of here. Beck's brother-in-law is going to find out where they're taking him. You can visit him in a little while and we'll figure all this out."

"Thanks." Maryn allowed Alyssa to pull her into a hug, but she couldn't feel anything but the chill and the fear.

Tucker was afraid and the unjustness of the situation made him want to lash out. He strode between a circle of policemen and felt like he'd reverted to childhood. Misunderstood, accused of something he didn't do so one of the other children in the house wouldn't get a tongue-lashing or worse. He forced himself to stay straight and tall as cameras flashed around him. He really didn't care where the paparazzi plastered his picture, but he didn't want them to exploit Maryn.

Ah, Maryn. What must she be thinking? Did any part of her believe it might be true?

Murder? What in the world? The children he'd murdered in Afghanistan flashed before his eyes, but he knew he'd never be arrested for that. It was classified Army information and he had been under orders to do exactly what he did. Maybe this was his penance for following those orders so long ago.

"Who did they claim I murdered?" Tucker asked the redheaded policeman as they reached the car.

"Jaron Underwood."

Tucker shook his head, the name didn't sound at all familiar.

"And how?"

"You might want to wait and talk with your lawyer present."

"I just want to know how."

"Bar fight."

Tucker arched an eyebrow. He didn't visit bars and though he did enjoy his gym in Laguna Beach where he could spar with someone occasionally, he hadn't been in a real fight since junior high school.

The policeman escorted him into the car. "Watch your head, sir."

"Thank you," he murmured. He leaned back against the stiff seat. He'd call Johnson with his one phone call and let him get the legal team here. This had to be some awful mistake. He almost smiled as he thought of how upset his PR team was going to be.

Chapter Nineteen

Maryn waited hours with Alyssa and Beck in the stark waiting area of the Orange County Jail. They saw Johnson and Braxton for a few minutes, but they were working with the lawyers and police to try to get to the bottom of this.

Finally, they got news that she could talk to Tuck for a few minutes. Everything the officer said about arraignment and bail blew over her head as all she could think about was Tuck. At least they were allowing her to see him. Beck and Alyssa followed close behind. The officer escorted them down several halls and then into a room with an arrangement of tables and chairs. Beck and Alyssa waited in the hallway. Alyssa gave her an encouraging smile. Although she appreciated her friend's support, Maryn couldn't return the smile.

She sat in the chair the officer indicated and waited with hands clasped together to try to control the shaking. Tuck walked in wearing an orange jumpsuit, handcuffed and chained to shackes on his feet. It looked like he'd already been convicted and sentenced.

Maryn gulped and tried to plaster a smile on her face. "Oh, Tuck."

The guard sat him across the table from her then stepped back. Tuck's eyes swept over her. He blinked and looked down at his manacled hands. "I didn't want you to see me like this."

"Tuck." She reached out a hand to him, but a warning look from the guard had her pulling it back. "You didn't do this."

"You sure?" He leaned closer and lowered his voice, "You've seen my temper. You know what I've done in the past."

"Your temper?" She scoffed, glancing at the guard and officer who were talking and far enough away they couldn't overhear. "You got upset when I intruded on your personal life and as I recall you didn't even touch me or try to hurt me. And what you've done in the past is the Army's fault, not yours."

"I can't help but wonder if this is penance for what I've done."

"The Lord doesn't work like that Tuck. He forgives and loves. You've done your penance, it's time to move past that."

He glanced at her with a wistful expression.

"You're an amazing man, Tucker Shaffer. I know it and the Lord knows it too." She reached over and squeezed his arm. The guard was going to have to pull her away if he didn't want her touching Tuck. "This is all going to be made right, and everyone will realize you couldn't do something like this."

"I don't care what anyone else thinks, I care about you." Tuck stared deeply into her eyes and time seemed to stand still. She ran her hand down his arm, avoiding the handcuffs, and wrapped her hand around his.

"Will you wait for me, Maryn?" he asked, his voice gruff but his dark eyes tender.

"Till I'm puckered and bald, Tuck."

He gave her a smile.

The guard marched over to them. "Time to go."

The guard grabbed Tuck's elbow and Tuck stood. His hand was pulled from hers. She watched him shuffle away, so opposite his usual confident stride, and couldn't stop the tears tracing down her face.

163

Chapter Twenty

It was after two in the morning when they left the jail with a promise from Johnson that he would contact them as soon as he knew something. The arraignment would probably be in the late morning. Tuck had a team of lawyers meeting with him and the policemen, and doing research on the bar fight. Maryn could not imagine Tucker in a bar, let alone fighting over a stripper and using excessive force because of his Army training, which was the story they had at the moment. Supposedly the video had been on some America's Most Wanted website and someone had called in with proof that it was Tuck who killed the man.

Beck and Alyssa had convinced Maryn to leave, but it was a huge battle until she finally talked them into letting her stay at her own apartment. It was sweet they wanted to keep her with them, but she needed her own bed, shower, and clothes. Maybe she could get a few hours of sleep and then in the morning she could be there for Tucker. She knew there was no reason to sit at the jail all night, but it was hard to leave imagining him alone in a cold, metal cell.

Waving goodbye to Beck and Alyssa, she climbed to her apartment and put the key in the lock. An arm shot out from the darkness and grabbed her. Maryn screamed and yanked free.

"Shh, Maryn, it's me." James stepped out of the shadows. "Can I come in?"

"James." She sighed with relief that it was only him, but had no desire to talk right now. "I'm exhausted, this really isn't the time."

"I know. I heard what happened." He pulled her into a comforting hug. "I'm so sorry about Tucker."

Beck's sport utility door opened and closed and he hurried up the steps. "Maryn? Is everything okay?"

James released her, eyeing Beck's huge frame.

Maryn nodded. "This is James, my friend and editor."

"Oh, yeah, we've met before." Beck arched an eyebrow as if waiting for James to explain why he was there at two-thirty in the morning.

"I've been tracking her." James held up his iPhone and his find my friends app. Maryn had forgotten she'd accepted him and some other friends on that last year. She never opened it.

"You have your phone on you?" Beck looked to Maryn.

She felt her face heat up and had to resist reaching for her cell. Not carrying her purse tonight, she'd turned the sound off and hidden her phone in her bra. She should've left it home, but always liked it with her. "Yeah, I do."

Beck arched an eyebrow, but didn't comment. "Why were you tracking her?" he asked James.

"I just wanted to make sure she was okay after everything that happened tonight."

"How did you know?" Beck asked.

"Journalist." James lifted his shoulders. "One of those geeks who listens to police scanners. It's also all over the internet now. People took pictures in the restaurant. You and Tucker are both pretty well-known so it's gone viral."

Beck focused on Maryn, his eyes asking the question before he verbalized it, "Are you okay with him being here?"

"Yes. James is a friend. He won't stay long." She pinned him with a glare and he nodded quickly.

165

"Okay. Call us if you need anything." Beck turned and slowly walked back to his Audi.

James sighed heavily. "I get it, Mar. You're tired. I won't stay, but I wanted to check on you." He stared at her. "You need to know I'm here for you."

"Just like you were there last night when you left me with the bill?"

James blinked. "I'm sorry. You broke my heart, you know?"

Maryn was so tired. She couldn't deal with this right now on top of everything that was happening to Tucker. "I know, James, and I feel awful about it, but... I really just want to go to bed. Can we talk later?" She saw Beck's taillights pulling away. Alyssa must've convinced him that James was okay. She'd known James almost as long as Maryn had.

"I understand." He pulled her into his arms again. "I'm here for you. Anything you need." He tilted her chin up and whispered, "Anything."

Maryn pulled back. "Thanks. I'll be okay." She grasped her door handle.

"You can't seriously still want to be with him," James said from behind her, his voice full of contempt.

Her hand froze on the door. She counted to ten, but it didn't help. "He didn't murder anyone, James. If you knew him, you'd know the truth."

"He roughed up the guy I paid to watch you yesterday."

Maryn whirled around. Her eyes wide. "You paid someone to follow us yesterday?"

"Yes." James' blue eyes were sparking. "And your precious Tucker hit him repeatedly then told him to tell *me* to back off. I think the exact words were, 'Maryn is mine'." James harrumphed. "You want to be around a violent guy like that?"

The Feisty One

Maryn searched her mind and suddenly it hit her. Tuck had excused himself to use the restroom and been gone long enough that she started playing around with the paddle board while she waited. Had Tucker really hurt some guy? No. Unless he wasn't the man she knew at all.

Her back straightened as she glared at James. He only held her gaze for a second before looking away. "You're lying about Tucker hitting him." His squirm confirmed she was right. "And you had no right to pay someone to follow us. Tuck had every right to tell him to back off." A little thrill went through her. Tuck had seen the guy following her when she had no idea and he'd acted to protect her. *Maryn is mine?* Hmm. The thought of Tuck saying it was actually kind of sexy.

"You want some guy to claim you belong to him? Like you're another piece of property for his portfolio."

Maryn pressed her lips together. It wasn't like that with her and Tucker. He wanted her... all of her and she wanted to be Tuck's. Wanted it more than anything. The thought of him sitting in some jail cell stole her breath away. What if he was convicted? She'd never believe that he could murder someone despite what he'd had to do in the Army, but if he was convicted of murder... She took a long breath. How would she deal with that? Could she really wait for him until she was puckered and bald?

"It's none of your business what I want James. I told you no and you just can't handle that. I love Tuck." The words shot out of her mouth and she clapped her hand over it. Did she really? Love Tuck? Yes, she did and she wasn't going to let James make her question Tuck's goodness. "I'm on his team." She crossed her arms and gave him a saucy head bob.

"You slept with him again, didn't you? I know you two got a hotel room. Don't equate physical attraction with love, Maryn."

Maryn rolled her eyes. "If you don't stop accusing me of being a floozy I'm going to rip out your nose hairs."

"I don't have nose hairs. I have them waxed."

"Ugh! You are such a girl!"

James' eyes narrowed, but then suddenly they widened. Maryn heard soft footsteps and turned. A burly dude with no hair grabbed her arms while someone else shoved a cloth bag over her head. "What the Jehosaphat?" she screamed, struggling to get free.

"Thought you could con us, eh James?" A man with a smooth voice said.

"Don't fight them, Mar," James begged her.

Yeah, right. She couldn't help but fight. She squirmed and tried to get her arms free. When that didn't work, she kicked at whoever was holding her. The guy grunted, whirled her around, and pinned her arms to her side. She was airborne and her stomach plummeted. She screamed until a large hand was clapped over her mouth, cutting off her screams and leaving her with very little oxygen.

"Leave her out of this," James demanded.

"Not a chance."

Shaking her head to free her mouth and nose did nothing. Her head felt like it was going to explode. Her stomach slammed against the guy's shoulder as he pounded down the stairs. She was dropped into the seat of what she assumed was a car and shoved in. Bodies pressed against her on each side and then the door slammed and the car jetted off.

The body next to her on the right squeezed her hand. "Maryn. It's going to be okay. Just let me take care of this."

"You stinking idiot. What have you gotten us into? I'm going to kill you." She jerked her hand free from James and tugged at the bag on her head.

The Feisty One

"I wouldn't do that if I were you," the lilting voice said.

"Well, you're not me." She pulled it off to see the burly, bald dude pressed on her other side with a large gun in his hands.

"If you want to live, keep the mask on. The less you know about where we are going the greater your chance of being free again." He had some kind of accent, maybe Australian. He held out the mask to her.

"Please, Maryn," James said from behind the mask they must've put on his head.

"Fine." Maryn sighed and pulled it back over her head. "I promise you, James, when we get free if they don't kill you, I will."

The bald guy chuckled. James didn't respond.

Chapter Twenty-one

Tuck sat in his cell, head between his hands. Sleep wasn't going to come tonight even though he knew he needed it if he was going before a judge tomorrow. The police had questioned him with his lawyers present and his lawyers had done a great job of showing how little evidence the police had and how out of line the arrest was, but he had no clue if his lawyers were going to be able to get him out and get the police to drop these spurious charges. Being in this cell was the worse feeling he'd had in his life. No. Killing those children in Afghanistan had been worse. Watching the bear attack Maryn then seeing her suffer after had been worse.

He'd get through this. Somehow. Would Maryn really wait for him? He shouldn't have asked it of her, but he couldn't help it. Her response and the determination in those blue eyes eased the misery of sitting here.

The cell door clanged open and the guard gestured to him. "Time to go."

"Really?" He had no clue about the actual time, but the jail cells were still dark and it couldn't be eight a.m. yet. They had told him his arraignment would probably be later in the afternoon. Maybe the time had gone faster than he thought and it was morning. They could be taking him for more questioning or an early breakfast if his lawyers had swung a quicker arraignment.

The guard didn't respond or offer any information. They

walked past the cells and into a long hallway. Several turns later and he was led into an empty room. His clothes were on a chair. Tucker darted a glance at the guard. The guy actually smiled at him. The guard carefully took off Tucker's manacles and gestured to the clothes. "You can get dressed. I'll be right outside."

Tucker quickly shed the horrible jumpsuit. It was actually pretty comfortable after probably being washed hundreds of times, but he hated the fact that he'd had to wear it. His phone, wallet, and keys were sitting next to his clothes. Why would they give him those if he wasn't going free? He slipped into his linen shirt, loving the feel of his own clothes. Putting on his pants and jacket reminded him of wearing this with Maryn last night. Had it only been last night? Hopefully she'd gone home to get some rest. What a sucker punch, trying to win over a woman and having her see him get arrested. Maryn had taken it amazingly well. He wanted to be with her more than ever, but wondered if it was even a possibility now. What if he got convicted? Darkness washed over him. He tried to push it away, but it was heavy.

He opened the door, wondering if they let him get dressed to appear before the judge. He didn't dare hope, but still felt it in his chest. Wouldn't a judge need more evidence than one unidentified person's testimony, and a grainy video?

The guard gestured down the hallway. They walked for a few minutes, their shoes tapping the only sound. "Am I meeting with the judge?" Tuck finally asked.

"I'm supposed to let someone else explain that," the guard responded.

They turned and entered a waiting room of sorts. Tucker saw the dimples first. Johnson's grin was huge. Tucker took a step toward his friend then faltered. He looked at the guard who nodded to him. It was then he noticed three of his lawyers in the room also.

"Johnson?" Tuck asked.

Johnson hurried to his side and pounded his back in a manly hug. "They sorted it out." He pointed to their legal team, dressed in suits even though it was the middle of the night. They probably hadn't slept any more than Tucker.

The youngest member of the team, Tucker thought her name was Julia, smiled at him. "You not only had three solid alibis since you were in Jamaica at the time of the bar fight, but Johnson enlarged and freeze-framed the film and we were able to prove it wasn't you from the film they had. You have identifying scars and the shape of your lips and nose were different than the man in the film."

The police had shown Tucker the film to try to get his reaction. It had been poor footage, but he had to admit the guy in the fight was built like him and had the same longish brown hair.

"They also revealed who had turned you in from seeing the America Most Wanted footage, and the guy had reason to want you behind bars. The detectives said there was no way they were taking such circumstantial evidence in front of a judge."

That made sense, but who would hate him enough to want him behind bars? "Who made it up then?"

"You've been dating his girlfriend," Julia smirked at him.

"James?" Fire raced through him. He really was going to pummel that guy.

"Yep." Johnson nodded. "Slimeball."

Tucker completely agreed. "Thank you," he told the lawyers. "You're all getting a raise."

They all smiled, shook his hand, and filed out. He turned to Johnson. "Thanks, man."

"You'd do the same for me." Johnson grinned and gestured. "Let's get out of here."

"Sounds good."

The guard escorted them to the front door. "Thanks," Tucker said to the guard as he held the door open.

"Good luck, sir."

Fresh air had never tasted so good. Tucker simply stood there for a few seconds and breathed it in. He turned to Johnson. "What time is it?"

"Four a.m."

"Wonder if it's too early to go see Maryn."

Johnson chuckled. "You're so whipped, dude."

"I know." Tucker grinned and jogged down the stairs.

An Audi sport utility squealed to a stop in front of him. Tucker took a step back. Johnson was immediately by his side. Beck popped out of the driver's side door. "You're out?"

"They just released me."

"Oh, good. I was coming to see you, to tell you. I thought you'd still be in jail, but Johnson seemed pretty capable. I'm not sure what to do, but I think Maryn's in trouble. I called the police, but they didn't think I had enough reason to report a crime. Still Alyssa and I both think something's wrong. I woke my brother-in-law up and he's working with some officers to see if we can get some help, but I think we need to go after her."

Tucker stepped forward and grabbed the man's arm. "Tell me."

"I dropped her off and that James' guy was there."

Tucker's stomach clenched.

"She said she was okay and Alyssa knows James so we thought it would be all right to leave. But Maryn told him she was going to bed and she would only talk to him for a few minutes. I heard her say that."

Tuck nodded, wishing Beck would just spit this out and sick with the thought of Maryn being with James.

"After we got home, I just felt unsettled. James had said something about tracking Maryn through a find my friends app. I checked Alyssa's phone and she had the app and had Maryn on it."

"Okay." Ice pricked down his spine. James had been tracking Maryn. That thought alone disturbed him. He really didn't like that guy.

Beck thrust the phone out to him. Maryn's dot was to the west, right by the ocean.

"She's on a dock out on Long Beach?" Tuck asked.

"You think that James' guy took her somewhere?" Johnson asked. "Would she go willingly with him?"

"I don't think so," Beck said. "She was worried sick about Tucker. Alyssa and I barely talked her into going home to get a few hours rest. I just don't see her taking off for some dock in the middle of the night."

"Especially with James," Tucker muttered.

"You driving?" Johnson asked Beck.

"Sure." Beck gestured to the sport utility. Johnson jumped in the back and Tucker ran around to the passenger side.

Beck thrust the phone into Tuck's hands. "Navigate for me." He accelerated out of the parking lot.

"At least she still has her phone," Johnson said.

Beck glanced over his shoulder at Johnson. "For sure. I asked her about that when James said he was tracking her. She didn't have a purse or any... pockets on her dress."

Tuck looked at him sharply. "Where was her phone?"

"She said she had it. I assume in her bra?"

Tuck's gut tightened. Nobody better find that phone. "Did you try to call her?"

"Yes. She didn't answer."

"Let's not try again, in case it does ring and James finds it."

"Do you really think it's James?" Johnson asked.

"That's who she was with," Beck pointed out, cruising onto the interstate headed west.

"Yeah, but an old boyfriend doesn't kidnap a girl and take her to an industrial dock. He might try to force her into her apartment or something like that."

Tuck nodded at his friend, even though James had set him up to go to prison, it didn't seem logical for him to kidnap Maryn.

"Do you have weapons?" Johnson asked Beck.

"No."

"We'd better swing by our place," Johnson said.

Tucker nodded his agreement. He hated to take the extra time, but he wanted to be prepared. Nobody was going to hurt Maryn. He started praying that no one already had.

Chapter Twenty-one

Their hoods were finally removed after they were hustled from the car and into a building that smelled like rotten fish. Maryn looked around, her eyes adjusting quickly to the poorly lit interior. It was some kind of warehouse, reminding her of the spot the bad guys might hang out in a James Bond movie. This was not good. Her spine was tingling and her legs unsteady. If her pulse accelerated any more she'd probably have a heart attack.

The three men who brought them in escorted them toward a small office. The big baldy stayed by her side while the other two stayed close to James.

An average-size guy with dark hair, bright blue eyes, and a huge nose walked out of the office door. He glanced over her once before focusing on James. "Did it really need to come to this?"

James shook his head. "It was a mistake. I'll get it fixed."

"Why did you bring the girl along?" he directed toward Baldy.

"Thought it would be good insurance to get him to follow through," Baldy answered.

"And now if he doesn't follow through her death is on your hands too."

Maryn's hands trembled and cold sweat trickled down her bra. She felt her cell phone vibrate with an incoming text. Maybe she could ask to go to the bathroom and call the police? She stood straighter. "Let me go and you might not all burn in hell," she said in what she hoped was a commanding voice.

"Tell your girlfriend to shut it," the head honcho told James.

"Ha! He's not my boyfriend, my boyfriend is Tucker Shaffer and when he finds you he's going to make you all wish you'd never seen me."

"Tucker Shaffer?" Head Honcho looked at Baldy. "Isn't that the rich guy that got arrested for a bar fight?"

"Yeah." Baldy smirked at her. "Huge threat since he's in prison."

"Maryn." James squeezed her arm. "Stop. Let me handle this."

"Handle this!" Maryn shook him off and took a step away. "We're in this mess because of you. What have you gotten involved in, you idiot?"

"Your *idiot* has forgotten to deliver the latest shipment. He thought he could pull a fast one on me."

James held up his hands. "That's not true. My contact wasn't there. It was a simple misunderstanding. I still have the packages. Let's go to my apartment and get them."

"If it was a misunderstanding, why didn't you respond to our texts and phone calls?" Head Honcho glared with his brilliant blue eyes. Maryn had never seen eyes that cold before.

"I proposed to her." James pointed Maryn's direction. "She said no and I've been a mess trying to figure out how to get her back."

Maryn almost felt bad for James. Almost. But what kind of a dummy got involved with people like this?

"Ah. Love. Makes us into real idiots."

"It's the truth. Please. The packages are all in my spare bedroom closet."

Head Honcho tilted his dark head to the side. "I'm tempted to believe your lame story. I'll send someone. If they aren't there, you both die." He gestured with his hand. Baldy lifted a vicious-looking gun and gestured Maryn and James away from the office toward the back wall of the building. The other guys typed James' address in their phones then took off. Head Honcho went into his comfortable office while Maryn and James slunk to the floor, Baldy watching them.

"What are you involved in?" Maryn asked.

"It'll be fine. They'll find the heroin and then they'll let us go."

"You're dealing drugs!" Maryn got out, though her throat was closing off. "Oh, James, why?"

He glared at her. "So I could compete with your stupid billionaire."

"You're so dumb! It's never been about the money." She clenched her hands together.

"Keep telling yourself that."

"I love Tuck because of so many reasons that have nothing to do with money." Maryn groaned. "You honestly just started dealing drugs so you could compete with Tuck?"

James looked away, but finally gave her a slight nod.

"Oh, my heck, of all the dumb ways to get a girl. Now they're going to kill us once they have their stuff. We've seen their faces."

"Don't be so dramatic." James watched Baldy carefully, but the guy didn't appear to care about their conversation. "He said he'll let us go, he will. That's why they covered our heads to get here."

"But we've seen his face. You can't trust drug dealers."

James exhaled slowly, but didn't respond. Maryn's entire body was trembling. James put an arm around her. She wanted to elbow him in the gut, but she needed something to hold on to right now or a full meltdown would commence. If she ran screaming, would they shoot her? Then she remembered. Her phone. There was hope.

"Um, sir," she said to Baldy. "Do you have a restroom?"

178

"Nope."

"Um, could I borrow some napkins and go around back?"

He chuckled. "No. You can go right there for all I care."

"And ruin this dress?"

His eyes flicked over her and she felt like she'd just rolled in the mud and would never be clean again. "I can help you out of it if you'd like."

Maryn folded her arms across her chest and looked away. James pulled her closer. "Mar. Please stop talking."

She burrowed her head into his chest. "I've got my cell phone in my bra."

They'd taken James' phone on the car ride over, but she'd told them hers was in her purse at her house.

"I wondered where it was."

"Do you think I dare try to call 911?"

James watched Baldy for a few seconds. "Not right now, but maybe he'll get distracted or bored watching us soon."

At least James didn't discourage her from calling for help. He would be arrested right along with these other scumbags. She felt bad about that, but he was the one who had started dealing drugs. Thinking about arrest brought her back to Tucker. The thought of him sitting in a prison cell turned her stomach worse than the rotten fish stench in this place. She started praying, *Please bless Tucker can get free and please bless these guys won't kill us.*

Maryn heard a vehicle pull up outside then the soft tapping of feet walking toward the warehouse. Her stomach tightened. The other bad dudes were back. Even if they found the drugs James had hidden, would they really let them go?

She didn't see anyone in the dim interior. Then suddenly a gun was pointed at Baldy's head. "Drop the weapon," a voice said.

Baldy complied. Johnson stepped forward and kicked the gun out of the way.

"Johnson," Maryn cried out then clapped her hand over her mouth. She looked to the office, but Head Honcho didn't appear.

Johnson smiled at her and brought a finger to his lips. "Lay down nice and easy."

Baldy nodded and lay face down.

"You know this guy?" James asked.

"Yes. He's Tucker's best friend."

Tucker came out of the gloom with a rifle in his right hand.

"Tucker!" Maryn gasped, thankfully a little quieter this time. She sprang to her feet and threw herself into his arms. "How'd you get free? How'd you find us?"

Tucker silenced her with a quick kiss to her lips. Maryn clung to him, joy radiating through her. Johnson finished tying Baldy's wrists and ankles then attached them together with a thick rope.

James stood. Tucker leveled his gun on him. "As far as I'm concerned you're one of them."

"I'm not," James protested.

"Don't make me think otherwise," Tucker said.

"Okay." James bowed his head as if trying to look humble, but the venomous look he pinned on Tucker said he was far from it.

"How many other guys?" Tucker asked.

"I think just Head Honcho in the office," Maryn said. "The other two went to get the drugs from James' apartment."

Tucker arched an eyebrow at James.

"They usually have a couple guarding the warehouse," James said.

Tucker nodded. "We took care of them. Let's get out of here. We can call in the location to the police once Maryn's safe."

The Feisty One

"Come on," Johnson said. "It'd be fun to take out Head Honcho for old time's sake."

"No." Tucker shook his head. "I'm not risking Maryn."

Johnson winked at her. "Way to spoil all my fun."

She almost laughed. The relief of being safe and Tucker being here made her so weak she leaned heavily into him.

Tucker kept his left arm around Maryn's waist and ushered her in the shadows toward the doorway. The door burst open from the outside and Beck walked in with his hands held high. The two thugs who were with Baldy earlier came in behind him. One had a gun jammed between Beck's shoulder blades.

"Shawn!" one of them yelled.

Head Honcho came out of his office. Tucker pushed Maryn behind him and aimed his gun at Head Honcho. Johnson pointed his rifle at the guy who held Beck.

Maryn was too scared to talk. Beck, here? He couldn't get hurt. Alyssa would never recover.

"We just want the girl," Tucker said. "Let us go now and I won't shoot you."

Head Honcho laughed. "You're outnumbered and you're making demands?"

Tucker inclined his head toward Johnson. "Did we not take out two losers outside and tie up the guy who was guarding Maryn? Plus, the fact we're trained military snipers. Johnson will take out those two, but you won't see that because of the hole you'll have in your own head."

Head Honcho's lips thinned. His nose seemed even bigger. Maryn stayed behind Tuck not daring to move or hardly breathe.

"Then why don't you do it?" Head Honcho challenged.

"This woman is all I care about," Tucker said. "I'm not risking her."

Maryn clung to Tucker, overwhelmed that he was really here and willing to protect her no matter what.

Head Honcho nodded, eyeing Tuck as he thought over his options. "So we let you three go with the girl and you leave James for me to deal with? How do I know you won't call the police the second you leave?"

"You don't. I'd suggest you move your operation."

"Killing you seems easier."

"Not if I kill you first." Tucker's finger rested on the trigger.

"Good point. Did you find the packages at James' apartment?" he asked the guy next to Beck.

"No. There was nothing there."

"What!" James screamed out. "They're there. I promise you."

"Quiet!" Head Honcho commanded. He held up a hand and peered out the door.

Maryn noticed the red and blue flashing lights. Head Honcho raised his pistol. The guy pointing the gun at Beck spun around to see what his boss was looking at.

"Down, Beck!" Johnson screamed.

Beck dropped to the floor kicking at the feet of the guy with the gun. Johnson fired, his shot hitting the other drug dealer and throwing him against the wall. Tucker pushed Maryn to the ground then turned and shot at Head Honcho, but the guy had disappeared.

James fell to the ground, covering his head and shrieking. Beck was wrestling with the gunman.

"Stay down," Tuck told Maryn.

She nodded, too afraid to move.

He sprinted toward Beck and the gunman while Johnson took off for the back of the warehouse where Head Honcho had disappeared. Tuck dove and knocked the guy off Beck. He pinned him to the ground as police filtered into the room. Tuck hauled the guy up then handed him over to the police. Johnson dragged Head Honcho out of the back of the warehouse, grinning and telling the guy to stop whining.

Maryn saw a flash of silver in Head Honcho's hand. Tucker was quicker than her ability to even scream a warning to Johnson, running at Head Honcho and knocking away the knife that almost speared into Johnson's abdomen. The knife clattered to the floor as the police ran to wrench Head Honcho from Johnson's clasp.

Johnson heaved a sigh of relief. "I didn't even see that coming. Thanks, man."

Tucker nodded. Maryn could see that his hands were trembling slightly.

James stood, looking around with wild eyes.

"Don't do it, James," Maryn said, standing to face him. "Don't run. They'll catch you and it'll be much worse."

James focused on her and shook his head. "I can't go to prison, Maryn, I can't."

Tuck came past Maryn on her right and plowed into James, knocking him to the ground with one punch. James screamed and rolled into a ball. Tucker jumped up and yanked James to his feet. "But you'd let me go to prison? The police know all about you, James. It's called falsifying evidence."

"No," James whined. "It wasn't like that. I thought it was you in that video. I was just trying to protect Maryn."

"How could you?" Maryn muttered to James. He wasn't the person she thought he was and because of his warped sense of love for her, he'd turned into a drug dealer and had Tucker thrown in prison. It was too awful to comprehend.

"I did it for you," he said.

"No, you didn't." She glared at him. "You did it for yourself."

He dropped his gaze and didn't respond.

The redhead police officer that arrested Tuck came and grabbed James' arm. "Well, this is a reversal." He tipped his chin down to Maryn. "Ma'am. You okay?"

"Yes," Maryn whispered. Not really sure at the moment. James had set Tuck up? Had gotten him arrested? An acrylic taste in her mouth warned her she was going to be sick. She fell to her knees and vomited. Strong hands wrapped around her and held her hair back. When she was finished, she spit and felt disgusting and embarrassed, but mostly angry at James. How could he do all of this to her when he claimed to love her?

Tucker helped her to her feet and tenderly wiped her lips clean then wiped his hand on his pants. "You okay?"

She fell against him. "Yes, no, not really. Just hold me, please?"

"I can do that." He tenderly rubbed her back and held her close.

Johnson and Beck walked over to them. Maryn forced herself to hold up her head and talk to them, though she wanted to just snuggle with Tucker and sleep for a few days. Tucker kept her close with an arm around her waist.

"Beck," Maryn sighed. "Alyssa is going to kill me for putting you in danger."

"She'd kill me more if I let something happen to you."

Maryn's legs wobbled. Thank heavens Tuck held her up. Tuck, Beck, and Johnson had all been in great danger for her. She'd never felt so loved.

"You finally convinced the police to come?" Tucker asked.

"When I saw you two take out those guards I was pretty sure this wasn't just James trying to get Maryn."

"Good job." Johnson thumped him on the back, his dimples on fine display. "And good job to you, too," he said to Tuck. "I didn't really want a knife stuck out of my belly button."

Tucker didn't smile. "I have nightmares about you dying all the time."

Johnson's eyebrows shot up. "Well, that's a cheery thought. Thanks again for saving me."

Tucker nodded and they all fell quiet for a minute.

"How did you get out of prison?" Maryn asked Tuck.

"Johnson knows better than me."

"They had no real evidence so the police were going to have to let him go anyway. Mama Porter, Braxton, and I were able to prove with travel documents, signatures at restaurants and the dates in his passport that he was in Jamaica when the bar fight happened. Then if you zoom the video close, which I was able to do with superb computer skills, you could see that the guy's nose and mouth were different and he didn't have the same scars, especially the one near Tuck's lip."

"I love that scar," Maryn whispered to Tuck.

He grinned down at her.

"Thank you. I owe you so much," Maryn said to Johnson.

"Well, if you ever get sick of the big guy, you could let me take you on a date." He winked.

"Johnson," Tucker growled.

Maryn wrapped both arms around Tucker's waist. "I'll never get sick of him."

Tucker kissed her on the forehead. Maryn breathed in the smell and feel of him, ignoring Beck and Johnson's amused glances.

The redhead police officer reappeared. "I'm going to have to take you all in for questioning."

Maryn groaned loudest of all. "Shouldn't we get a break? Because of you falsely arresting my boyfriend last night none of us have gotten any sleep." The sky was starting to lighten outside.

"I apologize for that ma'am, but we do need to get your statements recorded while they're fresh on your mind."

Tucker nodded and they all followed the police officer out the door.

"After questioning, we're going to your house and you're going to cuddle me the rest of the day," Maryn told Tucker.

He glanced down at her with an eyebrow arched and a grin on his face. "I'm in."

Chapter Twenty-three

Tucker kept his promise and held Maryn all afternoon while they both dozed. They woke as the sun was setting over the Pacific Ocean. Maryn yawned and snuggled against his side, looking out at the view from his sitting room. "That's beautiful," she said. "I think I could live here."

"You're beautiful," Tuck said. "Would you live here? Would you marry me, Maryn?"

Maryn sat up straighter. "Now wait a minute. That is no kind of way to propose to a girl. Nuh-uh. I need flowers and a beautiful ring and maybe some music, but most of all there needs to be kissing. Lots of kissing."

Tucker stood and walked away from her.

"Where are you going?" He couldn't fulfill the kissing requirement if he was leaving her.

"Just a second." He winked at her. "I'll be right back."

He walked out of the room and Maryn wondered what in the world was going on. If she was really getting a proposal, she needed to freshen up. A girl had to have dreams.

She ran into the bathroom and swished water around in her mouth then made sure her makeup from last night was still semi in place. She looked tired but not horrible. She found some toothpaste in the drawer and scrubbed her teeth with her finger. Feeling better and hoping Tucker was coming back soon, she eased herself down onto the couch again.

Tucker walked in with flowers in one hand and some kind of tickets in his other hand. Soft music played through the house's built-in speakers.

Tucker held up two tickets. Maryn stood and leaned closer to read what they were, but he kept them just out of reach. "What are they for?"

"Nope. I need a kiss first."

Maryn laughed and kissed him, grabbing the tickets from his hands as she pulled back. "Chargers and Broncos? Yes! My Broncos are going to kill your team."

He watched her with an amused glint on his face. "If you wear a Peyton Manning jersey I will claim I don't know you."

"You'd better believe I'm wearing his jersey. Peyton is my boy."

"Oh? I thought I was your boy?"

Maryn trailed her fingers down his chest. "No, you're my man."

Tucker chuckled, wrapped his arms around her waist, and softly kissed her. Maryn dropped the tickets on a side table, ran her hands up his chest to his shoulders and deepened the kiss. She trembled from his touch and knew she would only want this man, even if Peyton Manning came knocking.

Tucker pulled back, dropped to one knee and pulled out a ring box.

Maryn thought she might faint. "How did you? When did you?"

"I bought it two weeks ago." He grinned at her.

"Oh, my heck!"

Shaking his head, he said, "Maryn Howe, will you marry me?"

He popped open the ring box but she was already yanking him to his feet, throwing herself at him, and almost knocking him over.

"Yes!" she screamed, kissing him until he knew she meant it. Pulling back, she looked at the open ring box. The ring was a

188

beautiful round diamond set in a thick gold band. It was exquisite and as simple as a two-karat diamond could be. "Oh, I love it."

"You do?"

"It's perfect."

Tucker grinned, pulled it out of the box, and slipped it on her finger. Maryn studied the ring for a minute before looking back into his dark eyes. "I love you, Tucker Shaffer."

He swallowed and pulled her in for a lingering kiss. "I love you, Maryn Howe."

"I never thought I'd be grateful to be attacked by a bear, but I am. Otherwise I wouldn't have gotten to know you."

"'For my thoughts are not your thoughts, neither are my ways your ways, saith the Lord.'"

"What the heck?" Maryn straightened up. "You're quoting *me* scripture?"

"I've been reading a bit since we talked about being forgiven."

"I really do love you," Maryn said.

Tucker lowered his head to hers and softly kissed her. "I really do love you back."

Chapter Twenty-four

Mama Porter insisted on a celebration dinner that night. As they all sat around talking and eating roast beef, potatoes, carrots, and green beans, Mama interrupted the conversation, "Now, Maryn, I don't want you to go worrying that this whole crowd is going to be living with you once you two get married."

Maryn swallowed a bite of sweet carrots and looked at Tucker. "Of course you'll all still live with us. We're family." She had to clamp down on emotion as she said that. She'd never really had family and now because of Tucker, she would.

"Of course we are, dear, but you and Tuck need to have your own place and run around naked like newlyweds do." Her face colored. "Oh, my, can't believe I just said that."

Braxton laughed. "What Mama is trying to say is we'll see you often, but we're going to give you two some space."

Tucker nodded thoughtfully.

"And I bought the Hotel del Sol," Johnson interjected. "I'm going to be living there while I renovate a great house I found a mile down the beach. So you won't have to worry about me watching you running around naked." He winked and murmured, "Though I wouldn't complain."

"Oh, Johnson!" Mama Porter grabbed the dish of green beans and scooped some on her plate.

Maryn laughed. "Good. You shouldn't see that. The Hotel del Sol is a cool hotel," Maryn said. "We'll come stay."

"I'm in," Tucker murmured close to her ear and her stomach filled up with happy butterflies.

"Maybe you should have your wedding there," Johnson suggested, a twinkle in his eyes and his dimples deepening.

"Ooh, I like that idea. What do you think Tuck?"

"I don't care if we get married in Vegas as long as I get to marry you."

Maryn hugged him and laughed. "Thank you, lover, but we're definitely not getting married in Vegas."

"Hotel del Sol it is then. Thanks, Johnson."

"Sure thing. I'll have the wedding coordinator get a hold of you soon. What's the date?"

Tucker arched an eyebrow at Maryn.

"What's your earliest opening?" she asked Johnson, not taking her eyes off of Tucker.

Tucker grinned and kissed her. Maryn sighed against his lips as everyone else chuckled or groaned.

"I'll have them schedule you in as soon as possible," Johnson said, rolling his eyes and spearing some roast.

"Do you want to stay here in California or live somewhere else for a while?" Tucker asked her.

"I don't care where we live as long as I get to be with you."

"Oh, man, that's cheesy," Johnson said.

Tucker stood and took her hand. "Excuse us for a minute." He winked at Maryn and led her out onto the back patio then around the side of the house. Maryn tingled from his touch and his look.

"Done with dinner, my love?"

"Done with being watched when all I can think about is kissing you."

The waves broke and rolled against the sand, and the moon was reflected in the ocean. Maryn could only see Tucker lowering his head, smell Tucker's wonderful scent, and feel him wrapping her up in his arms and kissing her until she knew being Mrs. Tucker Shaffer was going to be the best experience of her life.

Additional Works
By Cami Checketts

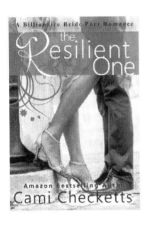

Also available:

Shadows in the Curtain

Dead Running

Dying to Run

Christmas Kisses: An Echo Ridge Anthology

Christmas in Snow Valley

Summer in Snow Valley

Spring in Snow Valley

The Fourth of July

Reality Ever After

Poison Me

The Colony

About the Author

Cami is a part-time author, part-time exercise consultant, part-time housekeeper, full-time wife, and overtime mother of four adorable boys. Sleep and relaxation are fond memories. She's never been happier.

Sign up for Cami's newsletter to receive a free ebook and information about new releases, discounts, and promotions here.

If you enjoyed *The Feisty One*, please consider posting a review on Amazon, Goodreads, or your personal blog. Thank you for helping to spread the word.

www.camichecketts.com

Excerpt from - *The Passionate One*

(A Billionaire Bride Pact Romance)

by Jeanette Lewis

"I, Erin Marie Parker, do solemnly swear, that someday I'll marry a billionaire ...

OR I will have to sing the Camp Wallakee song (with the caws) at my wedding."

The Camp Wallakee girls all ended up on the same row at the wedding. Erin was the last to arrive and was greeted with a chorus of squeals and hugs. She took the seat on the end of the aisle and shifted to adjust the skirt of her silvery gray dress. After brushing her rose gold hair out of her eyes, she leaned forward and beamed down the row at her girls. It was as if no time at all had passed and they were kids at camp again – sharing care packages from home, riding the zip line into the lake, roasting marshmallows around the campfire, and telling creepy stories in the cabin with flashlights under their chins. Erin's stories were usually the best, probably because she had the best ear-splitting scream and she liked to spring it on them when they least expected it. She always had to tell her story last because the resulting chaos would usually bring in a counselor who would yell at them to go to sleep.

Erin looked again at the row of women sitting beside her. Okay, some things had changed. The scrawny, scabby knees were gone, as was most of the acne. And they'd all filled out – some more than others. Lindsey was beautiful with her enormous blue eyes and pouty lips; Taylor was still tall and skinny, but not all arms and legs anymore; and Holly looked polished and perfect in her designer dress and chestnut highlights.

To her right, MacKenzie sighed. "Isn't this beautiful?" she said to Erin.

Erin glanced around. "Yeah. But who gets married in a cemetery?" There was no denying that the West Laurel Hills Cemetery in Bala Cynwyd, Pennsylvania was a beautiful place. The grass was still green, but many of the trees were wearing their autumn colors and the splashes of red, yellow, orange, and brown created a nice contrast against the blue of the sky and the white and gray tones of the mausoleums and gravestones.

The aisle between the rows of transparent chairs was a carpet of autumn leaves, ending at the Louis Burk mausoleum It was pure Roman architecture with its ionic columns flanking a copper gate, weathered to a gray green patina and featuring a sorrowful maiden in a dramatic pose that brought a sweet ache to Erin's heart. The wide, low steps of the mausoleum were banked with flowers in shades of cranberry, pale pink, and ivory.

But still, a *cemetery*?

MacKenzie laughed. "That's Nikki. You didn't think she'd pick somewhere *normal*, did you?"

197

Erin couldn't say. Nikki had always been a little quirky, but Erin hadn't been privy to her wedding plans. In fact, she hadn't known Nikki was even engaged until she got the invitation in the mail. They'd all tried to keep in touch in the years following camp, but some were better at it than others, and their contact had become less and less frequent as they got older and busier. Erin could probably have remembered what each of her friends was doing now if pressed, but she'd have to think about it a little bit first.

Which was part of the reason she was so excited for the wedding. Taylor's wedding four years earlier didn't count because Taylor had eloped and hadn't invited anyone. This was the first time most of the girls had been together again and it was the perfect opportunity to catch up.

"Do you know the groom?" Erin asked MacKenzie.

"Not at all," MacKenzie shook her head. "But I hear he's loaded." She elbowed Holly, who sat on her other side. "Isn't that right?"

"What?" Holly looked up from her phone.

"Isn't Darrin super rich?" MacKenzie repeated.

Holly nodded. "I think he owns some kind of software company."

"Count it," Erin smiled in satisfaction. "We never said it had to be inherited money."

"What are you talking about?" Holly wrinkled her perfect brows.

"The Billionaire Bride Pact," Erin clarified. "Remember?"

"I do," MacKenzie put in.

Understanding dawned in Holly's eyes. "Oh, that's right. I forgot about that."

Erin glanced at Holly's left hand, where a diamond the size of a small Volkswagen glittered on her ring finger. "I guess it's lucky you found Josh then," she said, widening her eyes dramatically. "Or you'd get ... *the consequence*." The Billionaire Bride Pact had been her idea - because *of course* it had - and the notion that anyone had simply forgotten about it rankled a bit.

Holly gave her a small, tight smile. "I guess."

"Do you know what these chairs are called?" MacKenzie said amid the sudden tension. She tapped the seat of her transparent chair with her long, pink fingernails. "Ghost chairs. Appropriate, no?"

Erin nodded, but her stomach was tight. Holly had always been hard to read and the two of them had clashed more than once at camp. Erin had had a talent for annoying her then and it looked like that hadn't changed.

She glanced down the aisle again, taking note of who was missing.

"Do you know if Kynley is coming?" Of all the Wallakee girls, Erin missed Kynley the most. Maybe it was because they had such similar personalities.

MacKenzie shook her head. "I'm sure she wanted to be here, but with her crazy touring schedule, she probably couldn't get away."

"What about Alyssa?"

"She's here, off taking pictures probably. Maryn's saving her a seat." MacKenzie nodded her head toward the empty seat at Maryn's side. Alyssa and Maryn had come to camp together; Erin wasn't surprised to see they were still close friends.

"What about Summer?"

MacKenzie rolled her eyes. "Who knows where Summer is? Probably sailing down The Vltava on a raft."

They laughed. If anyone could be found sailing down The Vltava on a raft, it would be Summer. "I'll bet she's wearing some funky bohemian outfit and has picked up at least one hunky Czech boyfriend, maybe more," Erin said, leaping into the fantasy.

"I'm guessing more," MacKenzie said.

There was a disturbance at the back and they all turned. The wedding party was getting into position.

"Don't you love weddings?" MacKenzie sighed, once it became obvious they weren't quite ready to start. "Holly, have you decided where yours will be yet?"

"Please have it outside," Erin urged. "Though maybe not in a cemetery."

"Ha! I'm getting married in the winter. Trust me, you do *not* want to be outside for very long in a Utah winter," Holly replied.

"But you could ride in on a sleigh, pulled by white horses," Erin said excitedly. She could almost see it. With her dark hair, Holly would make a beautiful winter bride. "The horses could have sleigh bells and you could wear a white fur cape and carry a bouquet of red roses, mistletoe, and *holly* berries. It's perfect!" She put her hand over her mouth and launched into her best Darth Vader wheeze, "it's your *destiny*."

Holly laughed. "Maybe I should hire you as my wedding consultant."

Erin shook her head, relaxing at the sound of Holly's laughter. "Not my gig. But I'll give you that idea for free."

They stopped talking as a pastor in a long black robe came down a side aisle, followed by a string quartet and a guitarist. The musicians took seats to the left of the mausoleum, while the pastor went to the steps. After a brief tuning, the guitarist began to play a series of chords and the quartet joined in soon after. Erin had expected *Canon in D* or some other wedding staple and was pleasantly surprised when they began to play *Can't Help Falling in Love.*

Everyone turned as the wedding party made its way down the carpet of autumn leaves, starting with Darrin and the best man. Darrin was not *quite* the kind of guy Erin would have imagined for Nikki, but he was cute in an understated way. His dark brown hair was newly trimmed, but still managed to look a bit shaggy, growing past his ears and long over his forehead. He had big, solemn brown eyes that made her think of a puppy poster, but when he smiled, they twinkled merrily at the guests. He was obviously having the time of his life.

Erin had missed yesterday's pre-wedding dinner. "Is he nice?" she whispered to MacKenzie as Darrin passed their row.

"He's great," MacKenzie replied. "They're so cute together."

Darrin and the best man reached the front and took their places at the pastor's side as the parents began their walk down the aisle. Next came Nikki's five bridesmaids in long gowns of varying shades of pink, wine, and cranberry. They were escorted by groomsmen in black suits with ties that matched the bridesmaid's dresses. Erin's eye fell on the second groomsman in line. He was tall, with dark wavy hair and was looking *mighty fine* in his suit.

"Check out number two," she muttered.

"Oh yeah!" MacKenzie replied.

But as the wedding party came closer, Erin's hopes evaporated. Number two was wearing a wedding band. Bummer.

The bridesmaids and groomsmen fanned out on either side of the pastor as the musicians paused, then started into the familiar *Wedding March.*

Erin couldn't suppress a squeal of delight when Nikki and her father arrived at the head of the aisle. Nikki's dress was ivory with a deep, V-neckline. The cap sleeves and fitted bodice were delicate lace that transitioned gradually into a flowing chiffon skirt. Her auburn hair was caught in a chignon at the base of her neck and covered by a veil edged in lace. She held a bouquet of creamy roses, accented with cranberry and pink flowers. Erin shot a glance at Darrin and was satisfied to see his mouth open and his eyes gleaming with tears as he gazed at his bride. Pure devotion. The way it *should* be.

After the appropriate dramatic pause, Nikki and her dad started forward, the leaves rustling and crunching under their feet. When she passed the row with the Camp Wallakee girls, Nikki grinned and shot them a wink.

The ceremony was surprisingly short and the pastor spoke only a few words of advice before leading the couple through their vows. Erin had expected something a bit more dramatic, but it appeared Nikki and Darrin were content with short and sweet. They hadn't even written their own vows.

After a long kiss, the beaming newlyweds turned to face the applause and cheers from the crowd.

"Ladies and gentlemen, Darrin and Dominique Pendleton," the pastor announced while Nikki and her groom shared another kiss. "The couple will greet guests here on the mausoleum steps, then there are docents available if you'd like a tour of the cemetery," the pastor continued. "If you prefer to skip the tour, there are cars waiting to take you directly to the Stratshire Club for cocktails and refreshments, then the reception will begin at six."

Erin and her friends joined the line that had quickly formed. When they reached Nikki, she squealed and held out her arms. "My Wallakee girls!"

For a minute there was chaos as everyone tried to hug and talk at once, but after a few minutes Nikki glanced at the line of guests waiting to greet her. "Listen, I'll see you at the reception, okay?" she smiled. "I put you all at the same table, so make sure to save me a spot."

They promised and after a final hug, they moved away as a group to the cemetery road.

"So what do you think?" Erin asked, eyeing the group of black-clad docents waiting for tour requests.

Taylor huffed. "No offense to Nikki, but I really don't want to traipse around a cemetery in these heels. I'd rather find some wine."

The rest of the girls agreed, so they piled into one of the waiting limos. Erin slid along the black leather seat to the front to make room for everyone.

"One down," she said in triumph.

"Almost two," Alyssa put in. "Holly's got her man."

"And Taylor," Lindsey added.

All eyes went to Taylor, who was staring fixedly out the window, even though the heavy tint made it hard to see much of anything. The unasked and unanswered question hung in the air. Does it count if you marry your billionaire, but then divorce him?

"Nikki looked so pretty," Erin said quickly. "I loved the way her hair looked with the ivory veil."

The girls launched into a conversation about the wedding, the dresses, the colors, the setting, and most especially, the groomsmen. Erin realized she wasn't the only one hoping Darrin had some wealthy friends. Though what were the chances they would all get to marry their dream man? The odds were pretty good someone was going to end up embarrassing themselves at their reception.

Her mind drifted back to the day they'd made the pact. It had been raining for three days and the camp was a quagmire of mud. After lunch, the counselors, evidently tired of cleaning up muddy footprints and trying to entertain scraggly groups of increasingly bored teenage girls, ordered everyone to their cabins with orders to *stay there*.

They played several rounds of UNO, Phase Ten, and Dominos, and Erin and Kynley did an impromptu talent show, but by dinnertime, everyone was bored and hungry.

Erin couldn't remember who came up with the idea of MASH (mansion, apartment, shack, house). Maryn handed out paper and they all listed four options for future dreams, including what kind of house they would have, who they would marry, where they would live, and how many children they would have. According to the rules, one of the options in each category had to be lame – like living in a shack, or ending up with two dozen children, or marrying a boy you couldn't stand.

One by one, they took turns picking a number and crossing off the corresponding items on their lists until they were down to one option each.

"This is dumb," someone, probably Holly, had finally said. "I'm definitely not going to live in a *shack*. My daddy says I'm going to marry a rich man and live in a mansion, end of story."

Erin had looked at Holly in awe. Aside from a few who attended on grants, the girls all came from affluent families – you had to be well off to afford Camp Wallakee – but the idea that you could *plan* to marry money, was new to her.

"Me too," Taylor had insisted.

"Let's all promise to marry rich guys," Erin said as inspiration struck. So the Billionaire Bride Pact was formed. They went around the room and each girl took her turn raising her hand and declaring, "I, _____, do solemnly swear that someday I'll marry a billionaire."

Lindsey drew up a contract and they all signed their names. As the years went by, they stayed in touch and eventually acknowledged that maybe *billionaires* was a little unrealistic. Nevertheless, they periodically reaffirmed their pledge to marry well.

And with Nikki's wedding, they were underway.

Read more or buy *The Passionate One* here.

Made in the USA
Lexington, KY
01 August 2017